Praise for *No Guns at My Son's Funeral*

No Guns is a desperate plea for peace, a search for answers to
a baffling reality. It is also a heartfelt elegy – for the youth in
Kashmir in particular – and for those in Sri Lanka, Israel, Iraq
– every troubled spot in the world where dreams are derailed
and innocence is sacrificed at the altar of bloody battles.

– *Tehelka*

…Voices from the valley that usually get drowned in the louder
sound of gunfire and political opinions or are often ignored
because they are still high-pitched, these are stories that don't
always get written about.

– *Hindu*

The tragic end to the tale is not a tear jerking sob story but
an eye opener as to the fallout of lives lived on a razor's edge,
driven by blind ideology rather than sane opinion.

– *Sahara Times*

… Paro Anand has woven a poignant narrative and a gripping
novel.

– *Hard Times*

No Guns at My Son's Funeral makes for compelling reading …
– *Sunday Pioneer*

WEED

Paro Anand runs a programme – Literature in Action – in Delhi and various places including Kashmir. She headed the National Centre for Children's Literature, NBT, India. In 2000 she helped children make the world's longest newspaper in thirteen languages in eleven different states in India. This is her eighteenth book. She has been awarded for her contribution to children's literature, including the IBBY Honor List for *No Guns at My Son's Funeral* in 2006.

OTHER INDIAINK TITLES:

FORTHCOMING TITLES:

WEED

PARO ANAND

IndiaInk
ROLI BOOKS

TO KESHAV

For your love, strength, and support
but most of all, for your confidence in me

 IndiaInk

© Paro Anand, 2008

This edition published in 2008
IndiaInk
An imprint of
Roli Books Pvt. Ltd.
M-75, G.K. II Market
New Delhi 110 048
Phones: ++91 (011) 2921 2271, 2921 2782
2921 0886, Fax: ++91 (011) 2921 7185
E-mail: roli@vsnl.com; Website: rolibooks.com
Also at
Bangalore, Chennai, Jaipur, Kolkata, Mumbai & Varanasi

Cover design: Supriya Saran
Layout design: Kapil Taragi

ISBN: 978-81-86939-41-3

Typeset by Bembo Roli Books Pvt. Ltd. and
printed at Anubha Printers, Noida

Contents

Acknowledgements

To all those people who took me to Kashmir, Lt Gen. and Vijaylaxmi Nagaraj, the National Centre for Children's Literature and the Rajiv Gandhi Foundation, especially Ratna Mathur. To the children of Kashmir who have offered me insights into their world and wounds and stories.

To Aditi and Uday whose love and support I can count on always. I couldn't have asked for more.

To Papa and Mama, Daddy and Mummy and Nano Bhuaji for everything that they do for me.

And yes, to Berna and Philo who put up with all my moods and fulfil every demand.

To Mr Butt and Butts Claremont Houseboats, where I found my solution.

Thank you.

I looked around the battlefield
and was amazed to see
the bloody pieces lying there
were all pieces of me
I did not know I had shattered then
into these fragments torn
each bit was lying so alone
So lonely, so forlorn

— Paro Anand

Before

Weed – a wild, unwanted thing to be weeded out. That's me – a weed. Not wanted, to be thrown out.

Left to fend for myself – if I must. Left to die – if I can.

Out. The word describes the circles of society in relation to me. Go on out. Get out. Out.

Out – wild, unwanted thing.

Protests of innocence. 'But why? I didn't do anything!'

Indignant protest. 'But why take it out on me?'

Defiant. 'No, I won't, why should I?'

Even helpless. 'Why me…?'

All gone now. Defeated, deflated like a balloon that's lost its breath. And so I'm banished. You won't be bothered by me any more. Not that you were really *bothered* before. *Before.* You won't even see me. Well, you may, out of the corner of your eye. That shadow lurking on the fringes of your 'normal world'. The shadowy figure that makes you clutch your purse a little tighter. Hasten your clicking footstep a little. Urge your beating heart, your pumping legs, not to break into a run. Away from me.

Yes, that is me. That shadow that you fear. The one you never stop to think about. No thoughts like, 'I wonder where he sleeps at night? Does he have a place to take a refreshing bath, a place to eat a meal served with chilled water and hot pickle on the side? Does he have a mother to say, "take care", or a father who'll scold him, hit him if he's done badly in exams?' Did you ever think while you tightened your hold on your purse and quickened your frightened footstep?

But, I'm being too harsh. Too bitter. Sorry, that is not what this is about. It's not your guilt I need, or even want. Why should I want it? I have enough guilt of my own, truth be told. Although, as I've said, *I didn't do anything.* No, I didn't do anything.

But my father did.

Tucked away in a sleepy village, cradled within the green arms of gentle valley slopes, was my home. *Was. Home.* A spring sprang up from the nourished earth. The snows were hard. But they always melted. We knew they would. And they never let us down. We were secure in that knowledge, even as we shivered against the colddark.

Now? Now I'm not sure it'll ever be spring again. For me. Ever?

The bakarvals brought their sheep to graze on the rich mellow grass. They brought with them stories of strange hairy animals that haunted the high hollows. Hollows that swallowed the light. As I listened to their stories, spellbound, drinking in their sour milk smell, I'd look into the high reaches of those mountains and long to be there. Some day.

Well, that day came sooner than any of us expected. Or

2

wanted. It sprang up from the slush of the thawing valley. Ready or not, it grabbed me by the neck and dragged me up to the dark hollows that held animals and swallowed light. And me. And now that I was here, I didn't want to be here anymore.

The cacophony grows louder inside my head. Blaring, shouting away the gentle voices of life's memories. The smells snuffed out by acrid smokesmell. Sour. Bitter. Not sweet like the bakarval's milky smell that clung to their sun-roughed, bearded presence. Ripped out. Not allowed to have sweet memories. Not aloud.

And I didn't even *do* anything. Ah yes, my father did. And aren't sons forever following in their father's footsteps? Even if those footsteps are blighted? So, this weed, filled with bitter bad blood, was cast out. To follow in his father's footsteps.

All right, I'll share my secret with you. My deepest darkest secret. I loved my father. There, I've said it. I'm sorry that I did. Love him, I mean. That I still do. But what could I do? I loved him. Like sons love their fathers, I too loved mine. I don't know if he loved me back. Now I'll never know. We were never that kind of family who express their feelings openly to each other. Not the men anyway. But he treated me like a man. And I loved him for that. I loved other things as well, like the tobacco smell that hung about his shawl – the dusty brown one that embraced him whenever he was most relaxed, its folds clinging to his tired limbs as he closed his secret eyes. Yes, his secret eyes. The smokescreen on his eyes never let you look in too long. Or too deep. He'd close his eyes if he saw you looking. As if uneasy that you could look in too deep. What secrets did he hold? I never knew then. He never told us what he did. Said we were better off that way. He never told me. But he didn't need to, in the end we got to know.

I stole after him one night. I had to know. Other boys in my class would share news about their fathers. 'He's got a promotion – we're going to be rich.' 'My father's new boss is a graduate from America. He says my father may be posted there some day. We'll all go.'

'Papa, what do you do?' 'Beta, I am a soldier. I work for the good of everybody. Not like your friends' fathers who only look after their own pockets and stomachs.'

But when I repeated this to my friends, they laughed in my face and said that I shouldn't be talking about my father with such pride. When they laughed at my father, I should have fought back. I should have scratched their faces, pulled their tongues out. Who were they to laugh at my father? *My* father! But I didn't. I turned away. I didn't do anything to my friends. I let them laugh. I let them make fun of me and my father.

My friends. They knew, but I didn't. No, I didn't even guess. Maybe I didn't want to. Or did I? Looking back now, I wonder. Did I know? Was that why I didn't fight them? Didn't challenge them when they made fun of my father? Did I know – or suspect? Was it on a suspicion that I followed him that night? I wish I hadn't. It changed the course of my life. The curse of my life.

What's so special about tonight?

We were told to go to bed early that night. Told that we were tired, although we weren't. My brother whined and protested. My mother almost slapped him, stopping the accompanying whine that was going to escape from my throat too. My throat dried up. My tongue felt like sandpaper and I crawled wordlessly into bed and didn't join in my brother's rantings against the unfairness of parents and the irrationality of their behaviour. Why should we be tired? He grumbled. 'What's so special about tonight?'

That's what got me. His saying, 'What's so special about tonight ...?' Yes, what was so special? What was it that we were 'too tired' to know?

Pretty soon my brother wore himself out with his complaints and fell into a smooth-breathed sleep. He was oblivious to the sounds of raised voices. It was my mother's voice that got me out of bed. She never raised her voice against my father. And he wasn't saying much, just taking her admonishment as though it was nothing. But it was the sharpness of her voice. The anger that shook it chilled my blood worse than the chill of the October night. She never spoke like that. My tiny frail mother. She wept, yes, that was her style. She occasionally mumbled under her breath when she thought no one was listening, especially him. But she never shouted. At us, even – rarely. But never, ever at my father. He wouldn't take it. And yet, she was shouting and he was listening. I cowered behind the door, amazed by this unlikely turn of events. I was so shocked I took a few minutes to even register the words.

'I hate what you've become – can't you see that? Don't you even care that your wife can't stand you? Does it not matter that you can't look your sons in the eye? You can't answer their innocent questions – you hide behind lies and deceit …'

And he didn't say anything at all. He listened, head bowed. He should have shouted back. He should have told her she was mistaken, that he had nothing to hide. He should have told her she was a liar. He should have. I wanted him to. I even wanted him to hit her into silence. But he didn't. He held his tongue and hung his head. As though he *did* have something to hide. As though he *was* the liar she was accusing him of being.

So, after all her ranting, when he whispered so that I could hardly hear, 'I have to go now, I'm sorry, but I have to …' I went out after him. It was easy because she was crying, too wrapped up in her own miseries to notice. Her, 'go then, go …' was lost to anyone's ears but her own. And he was too wrapped up, in his phiran, in his secret thoughts, whatever they were. He didn't know that not one, but two shadows left the house. Slipping away despite the curfew declared, yet again, a few nights ago.

It was the first time I was out into the colddark. The first time I saw darkness so thick that I had to push through it.

My hands froze the minute they touched the darkness. And the silence. I didn't know much about these things, but I knew enough to know it was very, very dangerous to go out during curfew. It was one of the things you just didn't do. At least the good, law-abiding citizens didn't. If they had to go out, they would get passes from the authorities. And my father was a good, law-abiding citizen wasn't he? *Wasn't he?*

So when did he start breaking the law? He who always told us to be good, always to listen to our teachers, obey our parents. When did it come to pass that he would sneak out at night, like a thief, a shadow slipping away from prying eyes? Risking the anger of the uniform that patrolled the valley?

I followed.

Questions pressed in on me. Those and the dark stillness of the night. There were no bird and insect sounds like there are in the movies. There was only quiet. Why? Had the night birds and insects also sensed the curfew? I would have laughed at the ridiculous thought but just then I stepped on a loose stone. The stone rolled, knocking into another and, before I could stop myself, I gasped.

I lay still. A minute squeezed past. Then another. Had he heard? Did he turn back? Or had he just continued? Had I lost him? The earth held its breath with me. Waiting. The quiet grew denser, if that were possible. I could not keep still any longer. Finally, I got up, cautiously peering into the blackness to make out where he was. I couldn't see anything. Nothing moved. Not a leaf stirred as I strained to figure out what to do next. I knew I didn't have the courage to follow if I couldn't see him. I wouldn't know which way to go. And I wouldn't know what I'd run into – the army patrols or those horrible terrorists everyone was talking about, abusing. No, I didn't have the courage to go on. So I turned back. I'd have to go home this time. But the next time I'd follow and find out. I'd be more alert and cautious. But when I turned around, I couldn't see anything but blackness. It was as if I was on another planet, or that I'd suddenly become blind. I didn't know the way home. I couldn't find the way home. What was I going to do?

A hand shot out of nowhere and stifled the scream before it had finished forming in my throat.

A cloth went around my eyes. My mouth was filthy, full of floury dust so I couldn't breathe and my throat was tight with fear. I was pulled to my feet, and then dumped over a man's shoulder, like a bag of garbage. He held my hands and feet fearing, perhaps, that I would fight him. But I had no fight in me. No strength, no breath. Only fear.

The hand that grabbed me, the arm that tightened around my throat was unfamiliar – hard, cruel. Like no hand I'd ever experienced before. Unrelenting. Bright lights erupted behind my eyes. My ears roared as much from fear as from the lack of breath in my captive throat. I was dumped into the embrace of dense bushes, their stranglehold combining with those of my captor. Tightening. Squeezing the life out of me. A thin light stabbed the dense blackness. I was caught in its beam. A gasp – shock – escaped from my captor's throat. The hand tightened around mine. He'll kill me. Whoever – whatever he is. He will kill me. Held in the beam, I was almost prepared to have the life wrung out of me, but not for the stinging slap that whipped across my face. What the hell? The roaring in my ears increased. The blackness completed its circle around me. 'Idiot!' breathed the man.

8

'Abba ...?'

Another slap across my already stinging cheek. But this time, it was suddenly familiar. The hand was not unknown, but that of my father ...

And so, I was dragged back home. My father in a rage so towering it seemed it would never end, never climb down so that our lives could never be normal again. It was the end of our family. As we knew it. It would never be the same again. Was it my fault then? Or his? Should I have minded my own business? But what was his business that made him lurk about at night, breaking the curfew? Breaking the law?

It came out. Like a wound so rotten that it spilled its guts and spread its maggoty stink all over our little wounded family, now breaking into bits and pieces. And somehow, when the break came, for some reason, I landed on the other side. On the side of my father. My mother and brother on the opposite. It was too late. In that one moment, it became too late and I was in my father's corner, whether I wanted to be there or not?

But memories may steal you away from the present into a world that doesn't, won't exist any more. I must come back. I must make it back from that murky moment. Into an even murkier present. The fog of memories sticks to my limbs, my bones. There is no way forward. There is nothing, until I relive those memories and keep them alive. To remind me, again. As always, the memories pour into the emptying vessel that I've become.

When did it become so bad, this situation? When was it everything took such a turn for the worse and started to dissolve into a spiral?

I was dragged back home that night like a pariah that had to be put down. Like a dog that had breached the rules just once too often. But what I had done was to follow in my father's footsteps. That's all. *He* had gone out. *He* had broken the rules. I was just trying to find out what it was all about. That's all. But I was dragged home. What have you got to say for yourself? Where the hell you think you were off to?

How could I answer these questions? I didn't know the answers.

My father had the answers, then why was he asking the questions? I should have shouted them back at him. *Where the hell were you off to, Abba? What the hell were you doing?* But I didn't. I just trembled, shaken into speechlessness. I had no answers to give to the torrent of questions. Except, 'I don't know Abbu, I was just ...'

But that produced a worse flood of anger mixed with – I don't know what. 'You never do know, you never think. Just do something so stupid, so dangerous never stop to think of the consequences. Don't you ever think ...?'

'So where were you going?'

'Who were you going to meet?'

'What the hell are you mixed up in?'

'With who?'

'Wherewherewherewhere? Who? What?'

The new man of the house

'I … I followed him …'

The silence froze over like a winter lake. Cold. The fire in my mother's eyes went out. The flash. The life. Cold. Like ice. Her mouth set in fury. I looked down and sure enough, her hands were trembling, shaken by an anger so deep it could not come out. If her anger escaped now, all would be lost, broken, beyond repair.

But her anger was not directed at me. Her eyes were fixed on my father. And he looked away. He couldn't meet her gaze. He wasn't sure which tack to take. I'd never seen him like this. He was the commander of our ship. But the power structure had suddenly changed. She had taken over. And she had only wrath. That and contempt. The mother's, the wife's heart had died in her.

But then Abbu put his hand on my shoulder, 'Umer …' He led me away and out into the night. We sat on the top step and stared out. He didn't say a word, but I could see he was deep in troubled thought. I waited. And waited. I glanced back towards the house. Through the window I saw Ammi sitting. Still. Frozen as we'd left her. Unmoving, unbending. She wasn't crying, she wasn't furiously tidying her tidy shelves as she used to when she got angry. Her tired body didn't even slump. And she wasn't looking out at us to see what we were doing in the darkness.

My eyes slid back to my father. He too was still. Too still. But his eyes were restless. Words pushed behind his tightly closed lips. I could see his thoughts. Almost.

'What is it, Abba?' Came out, rather than the 'I'm sorry,' I'd meant to say. But still he sat, silent. I couldn't take his silence any more. I couldn't take not knowing him – any more.

'Who–whose side are you on, Abba?'

But I now know that I knew the answer already. I just wasn't sure, any more, which the good side was and which the bad.

But all he told me was that he'd be leaving now. That my mother, his wife couldn't accept his chosen path and that he could walk no other. They had lost all common ground and could not stand together any more. I felt the words rise up in my throat. But we are your common ground – your children are your common ground and you are our parents. You have duties towards us. But I didn't say anything, I sat mute, listening.

He told me, quite clearly, he was leaving. Us. Forever. But I was stupid enough to believe it was just for the night. Stupid enough. Or hopeful; even though there was no hope left that night.

He never returned. Never came into see his younger son, or wife again. Never said goodbye. Didn't collect anything to keep him warm that bleak night, or hold hunger away. Or anything.

'You will be looked after. Someone will bring money to you. But Umer – and listen carefully, for this is important now…,' he stopped and turned and looked me in the eye for the first and last time. He glanced in at the window. He lowered his voice, leaned in. A secret: 'Umer, someone will deliver money to you. To you. You are not to let anyone, anyone know you're getting this money. No one, understand? Especially not your mother. She will need the money, but she will not take it from me. Just tell her you've taken up a job, or something.' He paused, looked carefully at me; I could feel his watchful gaze on me. He needed to know that I'd understood exactly what he was saying. And I nodded, for I had, I think. Then he went on.

'Tell your mother I'm sorry. Not sorry I had to take this road, but sorry she couldn't accompany me on it. You be a good boy, now. Umer, listen to your mother. Study hard. Look after her and your brother – you're the man of the house now. And someday, someday, you'll know your father was not a bad man, after all.'

... or words to that effect. I don't clearly remember. Perhaps I wasn't listening too clearly. Perhaps I didn't want to know. That I'd never see him again.

And just like that, he was gone.

I sat out there, on the steps, outside the house. The light burned on that night. Inside the house, my bolt-upright mother sat frozen. Unbending. She didn't glance out to see if Abbu was still there, or gone. Not once. Perhaps she knew, after all, he would leave this night. Perhaps she knew all along.

Day broke, spreading its cold grey light on the newly fragmented family. On the new 'man of the house' – who was so full of fear and foreboding. A child. Not ready to take them on. A child chilled to the bone by the enormity of his loss and the long, bleak October night. Alone now. A child. Me.

The empty shell of the day hung dry and dusty

Ammi came out and sat next to me. Put Abba's shawl around my shoulders – the warm, tobacco-flavoured, the comfort-perfumed one. Into my frozen hands she placed a hot glass of tea. It then occurred to me that she had let me stay out all night. That she had let me stay out in the colddark. This wasn't like her at all. She who always admonished me for not covering up enough.

'You'll catch a cold, you'll catch a chill,' was her constant refrain. But that night, she'd left me to sit out, bareheaded, barehanded. Freezing, alone. Or had she forgotten all about me? Was she so troubled, so lost she'd forgotten about me sitting out here? Cold. Alone.

'We will survive this,' she said suddenly, in a new, low voice. So different I had to turn to look at her to confirm it was my mother who spoke these unusual words, said with a determination I didn't know she had.

'We'll survive. You, me and Umed. If we can stay together. Help each other.' Then she looked at me. She turned me towards her. Taking me by the shoulders, she said, 'Umer, we'll survive this, we'll manage – if you stay out of trouble. You have to stay out of trouble. You know what I mean, don't you? You're not to go sneaking out at night like you did. You understand?'

I waited, until I was sure she'd finished. Then shrugged, nodded and started to turn away. But she took me again by the shoulders, turned me towards her. Hard, this time. And shook me. 'Say you understand – say it.'

'Yes, yes, I understand.' I shouted. And the door creaked open to reveal a wide-eyed Umed – his eyebrows disappearing into his sleep-ruffled hair. Worried. But Ammi didn't turn to look at him. Her eyes bored into me relentlessly.

'Say you're not going to get lured by those badmaashes. Say you're not going to have anything to do with them. Say it.'

I stared back at her. I'd promised my father, assured him I'd take the money he would send for us. Take it and use it to look after Ammi and Umed. But here she was asking me to do the opposite. What was I to do now? Whose promise was I to keep?

'Say it!!!' she screamed. Hysteria made her voice high and sharp. Her fingers dug into me. 'Ammi,' whimpered Umed, before shaking me by the elbow. 'Say it, Bhaiya, just say what she wants you to.'

And so I did, I made promises to Ammi I knew I wasn't going to be able to keep. Even if I wanted to. But I succumbed to her hysterical voice and the threat of Umed's tears. I promised to stay away from anything, anyone that would connect me to my father. I looked away, unable to meet her gaze, the suspicious glitter that shone there. It would become a permanent feature. But there was nothing I could do about it.

15

The empty shell of day hung dry and dusty. Neither of us went to school. Once the embers of the chullah died out after the morning glasses of tea, she didn't stoke them up again. As though the house was in mourning. As though our Abbu was dead. We had to make do with the dry kulcha and bakarkhani, the dates and chestnuts that stood on the high kitchen shelves. I stayed within the protection of Abba's shawl all that day and fell asleep in it, exhausted by all the events and the sleepless night before.

I sensed Ammi come sit by me. I knew she was covering me up. A little bit warmer. A little bit safer. She soothed the throbbing in my head, knowing the ache was there without my even mentioning it. I think I smiled up at her. At least I meant to, for at that moment, in sweet sleep, I was on her side. Wanting nothing more than to be a good boy, obedient and caring. I think she fell asleep curled up in the hollow made by my body. At least I meant her to.

The lie

Once sleep is shattered, it doesn't just unshatter itself and become whole in one night. The shards of that once smooth soothed thing break and fragment and tear and hurt.

There were shouting, banging, demanding voices at the door.

'Open up! Open the door before we break it down.' The thud made it clear that they were carrying out the threat even as they spoke it.

The three of us got up, dazed, blinking at each other in an unbelieving stupor.

'Mian?' Ammi cried, reaching for the light by her bed. She looked around for him, 'Mian …?' Then, realizing her husband wasn't there, was never going to be, she turned to me – 'Who? Who is it?'

The door was splintering already, the shouts getting

louder. The three of us leapt up, finally realizing that our worst nightmares were coming true. Not knowing who it was outside; not knowing which side was fighting its way into our lives. I called, 'Wait, stop, stop it!' And there was a moment's pause. Silence. Then, 'Open the door at once!' 'W-who are you?'

'The army, open the door!' We looked at each other. Was this good? Or bad? In the wake of Abbu's revelations, I didn't know any more.

'What do you want?' I asked, my voice sounding high, like a peeved child.

'Open the door!' the command left no choice. With one last look at each other, Ammi nodded, I unlocked the door, drew back the bolt. They burst in, filling our little home with urgency and anger. And guns.

'Where is he? Fan out, fan out.' Our house was being turned upside down. Unmade beds upended. Trunks opened. The lofts emptied.

'Where is he?' the military man shouted into my face. 'Where is he?' Another had Umed pinned into a corner, almost lifting him off the ground. There were more of them pouring in from the back door. Glancing out of the window, I could see our house was surrounded.

'Leave them alone.' My mother's voice was calm – amazingly steady.

'Where is he?' they just kept asking the same thing over and over, as if they didn't have any other words. 'Where is he?'

'I'll tell you. Tell you everything. Just leave my sons alone. Leave them out of this, its nothing to do with them.' She had command in her voice. Straight-backed, she looked the man in the eye, as though it was her who was in charge. It left him no option. He turned from me. The other dropped Umed into a shaking, sobbing heap. Ammi nodded to me, indicating I should go to him. I did. I obediently crouched on the floor, gathering him up into my arms, his skinny body curling into my lap. I looked at Ammi, squaring herself, drawing in her breath to spill the stink that had contaminated us all. I didn't want to hear. Didn't want Umed to hear. The truth. But when Ammi inclined her head towards the door, indicating to us to leave, I shook mine. No. We weren't leaving. We were all in this mess together.

'He's left us ...' I felt Umed's body tense in my arms. Or was it mine? His arms tightened and he buried his head into my shoulder. He didn't want to hear. I put my hand over his ear and pressed the other into my chest. But there was no stopping now, no escape. And she went on, sounding old, defeated.

'Don't, don't tell, don't tell ...' I begged in my heart, shutting my eyes to hide the tears that had sprung unbidden. We were always told that family matters were not to be discussed outside. And these were complete strangers.

'He's gone – he won't be coming back.'

'Why?'

'He ... he ...'

Umed moaned, maybe I did too. We were both holding on to each other now.

'Go on.'

'He has ... another woman,' her voice broke; she pulled her head scarf lower over her forehead, as if to hide the shame of it all.

'What?'

'What?' I echoed.

'She has been his … he has been with another woman for some time now. I have been telling him, begging him, to leave her. But he wouldn't stop. That's where he would go at night. Then … then last night, I fought with him, gave him an ultimatum. Told him he'd have to make a choice between her and us.'

She bowed her head. She sank into the stool behind her; unmindful of the clothes dumped there when the bed was stripped. Then said in a hoarse whisper, 'He chose her.'

The army man looked uncertain; this was not what he'd expected. He signalled his men to leave. They did – this time quietly, taking the urgency with them.

He turned to look at us. Umed was crying – soundlessly. Tears pooled into Ammi's cupped hand too, as it lay there in her lap. A few moments passed, and then he said, 'Madam, you're lying.'

She was up on her feet, her eyes blazing, though tears still wet her cheeks.

'How dare you – how dare you?'

'It's not another woman, madam, we know this. You know this. You are lying. I want the truth.'

'I would never …'

'The truth!' he barked. Umed flinched, jumping in my arms. But Ammi didn't.

'I would never,' she continued in the cold fury that I'd heard last night used on my father. 'I would never lie about such a thing. No woman would, mister. It's a kalank on my head to have to admit to you, a stranger, that her shouhar has left her, her children, for another woman.'

The military man was taken aback by her angry tirade. He seemed to retreat. To believe her. Even I did then. Almost.

He tried again. 'We have information. He used to sneak away at night. He was involved in the plot to assassinate the chief minister.'

She looked him in the eye. 'Well then good. I hope you will do your job well. Find him, do what you need to with him. Jail him, or better still, kill him. That way, if I can't have him, that whore who has ruined my life won't have him either. Good riddance is all I want to say. And now please, leave. There's nothing for you here.'

She turned away picking things off the floor that had been thrown there in the violence of the search.

'Umer,' she called to me, 'straighten the beds.' She carried on, quietly, as though oblivious of the man standing uncertainly in the room. I glanced at him and he glanced back. Strangely, both of us were on the same side, Ammi on the other. He made no move to leave, though. And I made no move at all.

Then, as she lifted the quilt off the floor, the kangri hidden under it fell and then smashed on to the floor. Scattering ash, half burnt chinar leaves and broken bits of the clay pot on the sheet, the quilt, some clothes on the floor. Ash-grey.

And finally, finally, Ammi broke too and started to weep. She was weeping out loud, sobbing, beyond trying to hide anything of her trauma. She collapsed among the ash-stained clothes and just wept her heart out. I immediately made a move towards her, starting to push a whimpering Umed off my lap, but the officer put his hand up. He indicated I should let her be for now.

I didn't know if this was right or wrong. How could I know? – I was just a boy, a child. None of this had happened to me before. How could I know what to do? I was almost glad to have got some instruction, even from this stranger who had turned our house upside down. I stayed and my brother climbed back on to my lap, looking sometimes at my sob-wracked mother, sometimes at me. I waited for further instruction from either of them.

It came. He indicated I should get her some water to drink. 'Umed, get some water for Ammi,' I whispered, pushing him off my lap, again looking at Ammi, a little scared to go up to her, but the officer nodded and, finally, I was crouching next to her, pressing her hand into mine, stroking her bent head. Umed was whispering, 'Ammi, Ammi, yeh pilo, sab theek ho jayega.'

With one big sigh, she rubbed her face, and pulled both of us close to her. She kissed each of us on the forehead. Once again, as though oblivious of the stranger's presence, she pushed us a little away from herself. Then holding both of our faces, looking us turn by turn, in the eye, she spoke. Her voice was loud, formal, like our teachers' when they're giving us our lectures.

'Yes,' she said, 'Yes Umer, Umed, you are right, my sons, you are absolutely right to say that it will be all right. Yes, everything will be all right. It will, I know it will. If …' She stopped, straightened her back, squared her rounded shoulders, and then tightened her grip on my chin till it almost hurt. Looked directly, deeply into my eyes. 'It will be all right, if, if we, you, stay out of trouble.'

I knew now what exactly she meant by trouble. I knew she was saying we had to forget about Abbu and all that he was involved with and all that he had become. I knew now he was a… ah, but that was a word never to be spoken out aloud in our house anymore, or even thought in the quiet of our minds. We were not to acknowledge what had drawn him out that fateful night. Not to acknowledge the root of their fighting. And his leaving.

Terrorist, atankvaadi, separatist? Or freedom fighter, jihadi? Which of these was he? I wanted to believe the latter, but my mother, my mother knitted the fabric of the former and wrapped us tight into the thought that he was not someone to admire. Not someone to become. And she would not tolerate any other way. Finally the army man left our house.

So, suddenly, in the space of a few hours of one night, my childhood was gone. Gobbled up by the departing back of my father. And I was man of the house. Ready or not, here I come. I wasn't ready. I didn't know where to start. Was I meant to start working to earn some money? Were there savings? How long would they last? Did she have any plans, any ideas at all? And so, the new 'man of the house' sat down in deep thought, sipping the tea gone bitter now along with his soul. Bitter and cold. Winter-cold, never-ending winter. She sat with me. Seeing us sitting there and sensing that he should not disturb, but troubled himself, Umed crept out from the backdoor looking for someone who could explain, or just comfort him ...

All right, I thought, I'll take a job; I'll be a real man. I'll drop out of school – and this thought was quite pleasant and brought a shred of cheer for the first time since the darkness had fallen.

She was having none of it. 'You'll not drop out of school, son. We'll find a way. I want you to study, to get ahead. We'll find a way ...'

'What way?' I argued, 'There is no other way. I'll have to get a job. Let Umed stay in school – he'll "get ahead" as you say. There is no other way.' I was the man of the house. It was I who had to make the decisions now, surely. Surely?

'NO!' she shouted, almost. Her voice harder, sharper, than it had ever been before. Just as the night had robbed me of my childhood, it seemed it had robbed her of her softness, her motherness. Hard and sharp. NO. And there was no arguing.

Family secrets, family shame

So Umed and I continued school. We were left alone much more now. Especially me. But even little Umed. Even his friends are friends no longer. They were warned by their parents. *Don't play with that boy any more … you must have nothing to do with him. Stay away.* 'That boy' as if he were a disease or something. As if they could catch terrorism from us or something. Well, let them stay away, let them be scared of us. It suits me just fine. Fine. But it was painful to see the bewilderment in my little brother's eyes, he couldn't fathom why his friends were so wary, why they pointed and sniggered behind their hands. So I started creeping up behind Umed's friends, catching them unawares, pulling them behind the tree where I was hiding and clamping my hand over their mouths, stifling their screams, subduing their struggle. Their wide, frightened eyes thrilled me. The look that confirmed their parents' dire warnings, confirmed in me I was worth being frightened of.

Umed saw me do it one day. To Salim, once upon a time, his best friend. Umed jumped on me as I held the child down. He hit me so hard on the back of my head, it made my ears ring. I let Salim go and swung my arm and anger at my brother. He was sprawled into the dust. Wailing. A thread of blood snaking out of his nose.

'Why d'you do that,' he sobbed, 'why have you become like this?'

He looked so small. Small and brown, like a dusty sparrow, sitting snivelling in the dust. I suddenly loved him more than I had ever done before. Suddenly, quite unexpectedly, I felt like a father to him. Knew I'd have to protect him, no matter what. Knew I'd do anything for him. 'I'm sorry,' I hugged him. 'I'm sorry, my little brother, it just, it hurts me that he won't talk to you anymore. That he treats you like something dirty. I can't stand that, d'you understand why I do this?'

'But ... but, he's my friend ...,' Umed's protest was high-pitched and it stabbed at me.

'Your friend? What kind of friend? One who will hear the worst about you and judge you, condemn you, drop you like a piece of dirt, too filthy to hold on to?'

Umed was crying in earnest now, 'It, it's not his fault ... his mother, his father ...'

'Yes, yes, his mother, his father yes, they told him lies about you. And he believed it? He was willing to give up on you without even finding out anything from you, without even asking you?'

Umed was quiet all of a sudden. His sobs subsided in a second. He looked at me, sort of puzzled, as if I'd missed the whole point of it all.

'But he did.

'He did what?'

'Salim, he asked me, he asked why everyone's parents were telling our friends to be careful of us, to stay away. He wanted to know what had really happened. He said he didn't believe my father was a bad man who had run away from the police. He said he wanted to be my friend even if his parents didn't. He said he wanted to be my friend forever ...'

We sat there in the dust, I knew he would tell me, eventually, what he had told his friend. And he did. He spat out all the details he knew. I was surprised he knew so much. Of how our father had been working for the Mujahiddin. He had become a jihadi. He had been earning good money, doing many jobs. As long as the police and army didn't know he was involved, everything was all right. But then they nearly caught him doing something, but he wasn't sure what exactly it was. That's why he had to leave home. That's why Ammi was so angry. She wanted him to leave it all. But there was no leaving now. It was too late. He was in, and there was no getting out. He was never going to return to us again. Even if the fighting got over, our mother would never take him back again. And that there was no other woman like she'd told the army men.

We sat in silence as he finished, but the tears started up again and the nosebleed too, was trickling, along with dust, into the corner of his mouth.

'And you told him all this – you told Salim all these details about our family?' I felt naked now, exposed, in front of everyone. Now everyone would know that the rumours were true. They had heard the truth from the jihadi's own son. I shook him, hard. How could he have been so stupid?

'Something going on here?' a gruff voice stopped me as I shook my brother. I looked around. A gun stared back. 'Leave the child, why are you hurting him?' The army man extended a hand out and lifted Umed to his feet, looked at the bleeding nose, looked into his eyes. 'What's the matter, who is this boy, is he hurting you?'

'N-n-n-no, he-he – he's my brother, he just ...'

The man turned to me. 'What's going on son, why the attack on your little brother, some anger you need to take out?'

'No, sir, s-s-sorry, sir. It's just ... I just ...'

But he wasn't going to let it go like that. He questioned Umed and then me. What were we fighting about? 'What has happened?'

'Nothing, sir, just a brother-brother thing, sir.'

'Where are your parents?'

He saw a look in Umed's eyes, he saw us exchange a look. He saw – something. He heard the silence. He asked again, 'Where are your parents?'

'Ammi's at home,' Umed said very firmly.

'And your Abba? Where's he?'

'At work,' I said, 'at work.'

'And where does he work?'

'In-in Pampora – he ... he works in the saffron fields.'

'And is this saffron time?'

It wasn't. I knew it wasn't. Did the soldier know too? He didn't look as if he was from these parts – from Kashmir. He was too dark, too curly-haired.

'He's working on the chilli fields right now. It's chilli season.' I hoped it was. I wasn't sure. Please let it be the season for working on chillies. The Pampora red chillies were famous. I

27

knew that much. Zarina Khalla's husband grew chillies and had grown rich on it.

Soon, he was gone. The army man. With one last look, what was it? A warning? Almost. He went back to his post, telling us to stop loitering and fighting like ruffians on the streets, to get home.

Umed held my hand and giggled into his free one, 'You're so good, bhai, so fantastic. How did you make it up so fast, wow! If I'd been on my own, I'd have blabbed, I don't know what ...' He was happy, thrilled, like it had been an exciting scene from an action-packed Ajay Devgan movie. I really needed to talk to him about this. He had to learn not to be so easily fooled. To stop blabbering. These were family secrets, not something to flaunt. Family shame, more like. But for now, he was happy, so I let him think his older brother was a hero. It did me some good to let him believe that. Even if only a little.

Mists leave the earth's lap

Gone. More gone than if he was dead. More gone than I thought possible. I hadn't imagined, even when he was telling me he was leaving, that he would go so far. So far away that there'd be no turning back. I had imagined he would melt like the snow. Be gone for a while. But then, when the seasons changed and winter came around again, he would inevitably be back, wrapped in his hookah kangri perfumed shawl. But the seasons have changed, the shawl drapes emptily when I draw it out from under my clothes. Ammi doesn't know I still have it. She has wiped out every trace that he ever existed, that he was ever a husband and father here. That he was ever loved. But she doesn't know I have kept my Abbu's father-perfumed shawl to wrap around myself in my loneliest, lowest moments. To hug it close to me, bury my head into its soft folds and pretend my Abbu was filling out the fabric. To pretend I could rest my head on the shoulder that once squared out the fabric. It makes me feel better. Sometimes. It absorbs my secret tears. But now, as time passes, the perfume of my father is fading. Evaporating. Lifting off the fabric like the mists leave the earth's lap. And there is really nothing, nothing I can do to hold on to it.

Times were harder now than they had ever been. There was no money coming in. Sabiha Khalla came sometimes, bringing food. It would always be cooked so that it would look like the sharing of yesterday's feast and not charity. But in some fold of the cloth that tied the bundles of roti together, there'd always be a little money. Left there discreetly – never mentioned. No thanks were ever given for it. None was expected. For that would be a confirmation of the fact that charity had been given. And received. And also that money had been stolen. For Hameed uncle was a stickler for rules. He had never liked my father, and now his worst criticism was confirmed. He used to try to convince my mother to leave my father – from the very beginning. But of course she would have none of it. And their relationship had deteriorated into nothingness over a period of time. Eventually, Khalla would sneak away on Eid to give us our Eidi or bring us clothes. Often they weren't new clothes, but those her sons had grown out of. Which was fine for Umed, but since I was taller than either of my cousins, didn't do me much good. Not that I minded. In fact I hated getting old clothes. Old things. And Abbu hated it too. But Umed loved some of the clothes that came his way. Jeans from Dubai, t-shirts from the US. But he was careful Abbu wouldn't see him in them. And it was certainly never mentioned. Then, when Abbu started getting us good, imported clothes, Ammi would occasionally sneak something nice to our cousins. Again, their father didn't approve of things coming from our house, even if they were hardly worn, or even brand new. Our fathers didn't like each other and the wives continued to be secretly close and us children fell somewhere in between. The wives were sisters so they continued to be close, naturally, and kept an eye out for each other. It became even more difficult when the truth about Abbu came out. He was Enemy No. 1. It was, 'I told you so, I knew all along …' for Sabiha Khalla. It must have been hell for her, but we were in an even darker living hell, we didn't have time to think about them. At least I didn't.

Our fees had to be paid at school. They weren't much, but now every rupee counted. Soon, hopefully, we'd be in new classes. But, then we'd need new books, copies. Umed's pants had already been let out as much as they could go. And his ankles already peeped out a good deal from under them.

Ammi would be out looking for some work, any job, while we were at school. I don't know if she'd been able to find anything. Amazing the number of important things we avoided talking about! We concentrated on stupid things like too much salt in the wangan, flowers in the neighbour's garden. Skirting around the issues that were pressing in from every side, threatening to engulf us.

'Ammi,' I finally broached the subject, after Umed was nodding off, 'Ammi, you've been looking for a job, any luck yet?'

'Oh yes, yes, there are one or two good openings. I'm just waiting for one more interview and then I'll decide which job to take.' She smiled, a too bright smile. Something was wrong. She was hiding something.

'What?' she laughed nervously as I continued to look at her. 'What are you looking at me like that for, my budhu beta?' She looked away, she couldn't meet my eye.

'What – you tell me what?' I demanded.

'I don't know what you mean.'

'There's something you're hiding what is it?'

'No, no, there's nothing to hide, now go to sleep. You've school tomorrow.' But I caught her arm as she made a move to stand.

'You haven't answered my question. What jobs are these – what kind of work are you looking to do?'

'Whatever I can find, na beta? I'm not educated like you. I've never worked – I've no experience …'

'You've worked all your life. How can you say that? You've so much experience in running a house, being a mother, cooking. Why, you've worked harder than all of us, Abbu, even.'

'Yes,' she smiled her smile, 'I have that.'

'So, what kind of job possibilities are you looking for?'

'The kind I've the skill and experience for, beta. As you yourself said, running a house, keeping it clean …'

'You mean …'

'… cooking.'

'You mean you're going to work in someone's house? Clean someone else's dirty dishes? Be … be a servant?' The hateful word tasted bitter on my tongue. I was standing. I was shaking. This was impossible. This was intolerable.

'Yes,' she spat out, standing, shaking too now, 'yes, yes a servant. I am looking to be a servant in someone's house. Whoever will have me. It's the only work I know. It's all your wretched father has left me good for … a servant.' She sobbed, the anger giving way to tears, 'Oh Umer, I don't know what else to do; how to feed you, clothe you, keep you in school. I don't know what else to do …'

'But Ammi, Ammi, you can't, I won't let you – you're too good.'

'There's no other way, Umer, don't you see?' We had the talk again, yet again. About me dropping out of school and finding a job. But she was having none of it. The same arguments, back and forth. Me saying if we needed the money now then it was now I had to work. She saying she'd rather be a servant now so that I could support her in her old age.

And in my mind, I waited, hoping somehow Abba's people would contact me and give me money. He had promised someone would come – where were they? I kept imagining how I would manage to give it to Ammi. I knew she would never just accept it. She'd made that very clear. I lay awake that night tortured by the images of Ammi working in some rich man's house. What would it be like – my ammi, washing clothes that were not ours, cooking food that she would not get to eat at all? Would they be good to her? What if they turned out to be one of those horrible families who rebuked their servants – were mean? And what if my classmates got to know that my mother was a servant? Suppose, suppose, one of them was her employer?

I sat up, breaking out in a sweat, nauseous. I couldn't sleep. I needed to cool myself. Hurriedly, I pulled out Abbu's shawl and let myself out of the house. The chill of November immediately made me feel better as it bit into my bones.

The disappearing face

I sat at the spot, the exact one where Abbu and I had sat that night, the last night. The night when everything turned rotten. I sat there, I tried to recall his face, the lines around his eyes, the slightly off-centre nose. I knew it all, for split second, I saw his face, but then, like a wisp of smoke, it disintegrated, merged into the surrounding nothingness. I concentrated. I quelled the sickening feeling that rose in me. Remember him, remember his face, I knew that face so well. So why couldn't I recall it now?

I buried my face into the shawl, greedily searching for his smell in it but it was faint. I was panicking. I needed him. I needed him now. If I couldn't have him, at least let me recall his face, at least let me have his memory. Give me back the memory of your face, I begged. If I couldn't even recall his face, his voice, his touch, his smell, then, then, all hope was lost. Please, please come back; please let me at least remember. Where are you?

Whereareyouwhereareyou? I didn't know when I started crying. But I knew when I stopped. Made myself stop. I made up my mind I'd try and reach him, send him messages. It could happen, I'd heard about people thinking of someone so hard and then that person knowing that they were being remembered. Just by thinking!

So I thought. Fiercely I sent out messages, 'Abbu, Abbu, we're desperate. Send us some money otherwise Ammi's going to become a servant. Abbu. Help. Money. Abbu. Help. Money. Please Abbu. Abbuhelpmoneyabbuhelpmoney abbuhelpmoneyabbuhelpmoney ...'

'It'll be all right,' said a voice, said a hand pressing my shoulder.

'Abbu?' But it was Ammi.

'Umer. I know you hate this thought; I don't much like it either. But I really, really don't want you dropping out of school. Your Abbu won't want that either, for you.'

'He wouldn't want this for you, Ammi.'

'No, Umer, you're right. He wouldn't. Your Abbu was a good man, Umer. A decent man. And that's how I want you to remember him always. But he always wanted more for you than he thought his decency could provide. He wanted Umed and you to have what his honest living couldn't pay for. And he was a weak man. I see that now. He wasn't greedy, not for himself. He was greedy for his family. And his greed made him weak. Left him wanting. And in this valley of ours, there are plenty of vultures who'll smell a person's hunger, sense his wanting, his longing. And they will consume him. Like vultures on a carcass, they'll strip him down to nothingness. To where his iman, his goodness, his sense of justice and honesty, why even his greed are consumed. He was a good man, Umer, but look at what his

35

greed has done.' She whispered now, softly. She was stroking her husband's shawl with a longing of her own, but when I wrapped my fingers around her work-roughed hands, she withdrew from the warmth of the shawl. As though fearing it might taint her with a greed of its own.

'So, you see my son, it is not for nothing I insist that you continue your studies. I never want you to feel that hunger, the need to fall prey to the vultures that lurk in every corner. I want you to have a full education, to get a job where you can hold your head high, walk in the sun, fill your pockets and fulfil your heart's desires. And if I have to be a servant to get you there, then I will − but not a day more than I need to, I promise you that, all right?'

'All right,' I said finally, 'I'll do as you say. But the day I get that job, I'll provide for both of you, okay? And you'll have to stop working.'

'Oh ho, the very minute you have your first salary, I'll be a lady of leisure. Then I'll need servants of my own − and not just one, mind you.' She giggled like a little girl and mimicked being a lady, stretching out her legs and propping her head up on a make-believe pillow.

'Ah yes,' she continued, obviously enjoying the images that played in her mind, 'I'll want one servant to press my legs and one to fill my hookah …' Her laugh was like birds flying home after a long journey out. I hadn't heard her laugh like this in a long, long time, not since Abbu had left. Before that, even. She was flat on her back now, gazing up at the stars crowding the night sky. A little girl's wistfulness in her eyes. Wishing for ease, for easier times, for 'before'. I took her hand again and kissed the open palm, 'But Ammi, you'll still cook for us, no? Your creamy yakhni, with spicy chonth?' She hadn't cooked much for us since Abbu left, nothing special, nothing that had encouraged us to take a second helping. 'I will, Umer. You study and I'll cook ...'

And with that we started our lives again. Ammi left after we did. She was back before we returned from school. So we didn't see her being a servant. We didn't talk about it either. How could I ask the questions that hovered in my head? How could I ask her, my own Ammi, what her employers were like – did they greet her when she stepped over their threshold? What did they call her? Were their children respectful? Did they offer her tea and something to eat? Did they set aside food for her before they ate, or did they give her leftovers, or did they not feed her at all? Did they know anything about her, that she had children, that she had a husband – once? I'd been trying to picture her day, but even in my mind's eye I couldn't bear the images and shut down on it.

So we didn't talk about her 'job'. We were becoming experts in avoiding important issues and frilling up trivial ones. Umed was probably also aware of what her job really was, but he never asked her. I think. And he certainly never asked me. Only once, at night, as we lay down to sleep, he'd commented on how tired she looked nowadays. I didn't know how to react. I almost blurted out my own fears and worries about her, but I didn't have the energy to go into a long discussion about it. So we both slept with questions disturbing our sleep. And when we awoke the next morning, we avoided each other's eyes and pretended all was well.

And we muddled around like that until Aman came into our lives and forced us to stop avoiding the hovering questions.

37

Aman

It was Asif who told me about it. And Sabiha Khalla who told Ammi. At the same time. It came to Umed's ears as well though he couldn't quite remember how — at least that's what he said. Aman. An organization that helped what they called the half-widowed and half-orphaned. We had a title now. A name to call our sadness by. Half. Those whose husbands had disappeared. No one was sure whether they'd been 'taken' by the army or separatists. Or what?

There were announcements made about it — how they were going to help people like us. Here, at last, was hope. Aman. Maybe we'd be free of our troubles now. Maybe this was where Ammi could stop being a servant.

So we went. We left Umed at home. No point him watching us becoming beggars. No need for him to know.

Ammi and I caught the bus. Both of us were confused by

the mixture of hope and embarrassment that whirled around us. Once there, we didn't meet anyone's eye – the other halves who were there. They didn't acknowledge us either. But, from the corner of my eye I saw each one's back was bent, shoulders drooped. I tried to square mine out. But that didn't last too long. We were handed a form and told to fill it up and then go to a lady who sat behind a desk sifting through forms of other destitute families.

We had brought our pens and started to fill in the details that made up our lives. Names of family members, number of dependents, their ages. Where do we study, classes. These were easy questions. Then there were ones that weren't. Date of disappearance or death of husband/father. Work he did, money he'd earned. Ownership of the house. Present income, if any. Present place of employment. It was all out in the open now. Even strangers knew of our struggle, our empty pockets. Our often empty stomachs and now, also the secret we'd been too ashamed to share, even with each other. The fact that our mother was a servant. In some home where they still had enough to eat, enough to employ someone's mother to wash their dirty clothes and dishes. The form was filled so we went to the desk to hand it over to the lady behind the desk. I watched as she read it, looking out for signs of pity or understanding or something. But the woman in a green salwar kameez had an impassive face and didn't show a flicker of anything. No emotion as we revealed our life to her. Then, finally, she signed at the bottom of the form – the sum total of our lives – and put it into an 'out' tray. Then she handed us a token with a number on it and told us to wait our turn. We were now not Ammi and Umed, we were number 272. There were going to be more strangers reading our dirty secrets now.

Staring out of the window at the winter-grey landscape, I couldn't help but wonder what compelled my father to bring us to this moment. What were those beliefs, those convictions that were greater than the total of us – his wife, his sons, his home, his job. His life. His history. His entirety.

I wondered if I could ever, ever be so, so sure, so convinced of something that I could give up my entire everything. I didn't think so; I was too – I don't know – lazy?

We waited. I looked down at our token. Number 272. What did the number mean? Were we family number 272. Had there been 271 people before us? Today, this week, this month? How many of us halves were out there? I was going to ask Ammi, but when I looked over, I found she was praying.

Our number was called. I was so lost in my thoughts I didn't even hear it. Ammi had to shake me out of my reverie. I followed her, feeling a mixture of dread and relief. Dread they'd ask more probing questions. Find out what Abba had really been about. Dread they'd find out more about Ammi's job, and while they were doing that, I'd find out more too. The questions hovering in my head for so long would be answered in my presence. But I didn't want to know. Didn't want to look at this truth in its face, not after I'd had my fair share of dreadful truths – more than my fair share.

But also relief, because maybe then some of our problems would actually be solved. The financial ones at least. Maybe, just maybe, it would be enough for Ammi to stop working. If it wasn't, well, maybe I'd ask them if it was possible for them to give her a job – something, anything would be better than what she did now. If the financial burden was off our shoulders, then maybe we could concentrate on other things.

But what was this? Ammi was being led off by some woman and I was being asked to accompany an official looking man in the opposite direction. Why were we being separated?

'Ammi ...' I went after her. Who were these people to separate us anyway? 'Ammi, wait ...' They stopped. The official looking man put an official looking hand on my shoulder.

'It's all right, son,' he said. I almost turned around to shout, 'I'm not your son, I'm Abbu's son ...,' but instead, I just ignored him and stepped up to Ammi.

'Where are you going?'

'Beta, they say they'll talk to us separately. It's all right, what can be the harm?'

'Harm? Of course there's harm.' I was really angry. Really, really angry. 'Do they think we're criminals that they have to question us separately? What is this? An interrogation?'

'No, no, son,' said Mr Official, again, pretending to be my father – a person who loved me, knew me. 'Please, don't mind. It is just that there are two departments: one for the widows, one for the orphans.'

I could have hit him, right there and then. In a flash, I could have given it all up, thrown away our best and only chance, just to hit him.

'We're not orphans,' I was shouting, 'look, look. This woman, she's my mother and she's alive. And our Abbu – our Abbu ...' I tried stopping myself. But I'd lost control. I was hysterical and I was crying. Everybody in the waiting area was staring. The ones' who wouldn't look you in the face were looking now – staring, for I'd only said what was in their hearts. This was rock bottom; we couldn't get any lower than this. Or so I thought, not knowing in my naivete, that there were layers, worlds beneath where we stood now.

So they questioned us together, after plying us with very sweet, milky tea and very large, very yellow floury, fruity cake slices that made me feel sick and choked.

One of them sat to one side and furiously wrote down everything we said. It really did feel like an interrogation, although they didn't seem to be asking very important questions. Questions similar to the ones we had filled in our form: what class each of us studied in, which houses Ammi worked in, how much she was paid, the work she did there. Stuff easy to answer. I didn't see why we needed to be asked these questions separately at all.

Then the official pretending to be my father stood up. 'Are you feeling better now, beta?' He asked in that patronizing voice of his with the fake smile.

'I'm fine,' I snapped back, 'I'm always fine.'

'Beta,' muttered Ammi, shifting uneasily in her chair. I knew what she was trying to say. We didn't want to antagonize this man. He was our lifeline – a way out of the pit in which we found ourselves. I took deep breaths. I knew I should not hate this man the way I inexplicably did. I knew I'd do better to calm down. He was just doing his job.

'Yes, sir, sorry, sir.'

'Now look, son,' I gritted my teeth against his 'son'.

'Son, it's part of the necessary procedure for us to question both of you separately. I hope you don't mind ...'

'No sir.'

'Good, shabaash. Now, madam, you please stay here and my colleague will join you in a few moments. And son, will you come with me down the hall, please?'

'Yes sir.' What choice did I have? His fingers burned into my shoulder as he guided me out. I don't know why I took such a dislike to him. But I was careful not to shrug his hand off. I knew he was trying to be kind and, God help us, we needed his kindness.

I sat next to him in the dingy room as he handed our papers over to another, probably a more senior man who sat across the table. For a few moments there was complete silence, filled only by the impertinent rattling of the polythene sheets taped across the paneless windows. But the December wind outside was not allowed in to freshen the dank air.

Finally, the man took his arms out of his phiran to look at all our papers. He looked bored. I suppressed a shudder of irritation. I suppose he must be bored. After all, he met hundreds of us through the day. The same sad faces, the same sorry stories.

Questions

'So, your father has been killed?' he finally said in a voice so flat and bored – as if he were asking, 'so, do you have a blue pen?' or something as inane as that.

I was shocked. No one had asked that. It had never been mentioned. I never thought he'd be dead – killed. I was stunned at the sudden possibility. Unbidden, images leapt behind my now closed eyelids. Abbu running, someone chasing him. Who? Who is behind him? Army? Police? His own people? Others? – who? Gunfire, shouting. He's falling – where? Into a river, on the road. The water turns red, there's traffic on the road, a big army truck. Rolling by. Is he alone in some desolate, silent place? There's blood. Is it his? Is he bleeding – bleeding to death?

'Idon'tknow, Idon'tknowIdon'tknowIdon'tknow.'

I don't know anything anymore. I'm crying, moaning and the man next to me is hushing me. But the bored man is unperturbed, unmoved. He's seen it all before. He's bored. He wants me – number 272 – to be out of there quickly so he can get on to number 273 and 4 and 5 and then have his lunch, then 6 and 7 and 12 to 17 until he can go home and have dinner cooked by his wife and play with his sons, content in the knowledge he is a person. Not a number. He'll never be a number, this man across the desk.

'Sir, his father is not killed – he has disappeared, sir.' The man next to me allows a hint of disapproval into his voice as he pats my hand as it rests next to me. But the bored man is too bored. He glances at the papers, mumbles, 'quite right', and then peers at me over his half-moon glasses.

'Tell me about the disappearance of your father. What happened? When did it happen? I want all the details. Leave nothing out. The more we know, the more we can help you.' His voice is nasal, he glances at his colleagues as though they share something – a secret, I'm not allowed to be a part of.

'Well,' I begin, 'it was a while ago, so I don't know how much I remember ...'

Ammi and I should have gone over this. We should have got our story sorted out. Then it hits me. This *is* an interrogation – that's why they only asked the stupid, obvious questions when we were together and insisted that we were questioned separately for those that would make or break our case. But Ammi and I were so wrapped up in our shame and misery, we forgot to get our story straight. And now it is too late. Too late.

The man continues to peer at me, steadily over his spectacles. He's waiting and I can't play for time. So I plunge in, spinning the fabric of my lies. Trying not to remember that my mother is not a good liar.

'He was taken. He was coming to pick me up from my computer centre. It got late because some of the terminals were down, so there was a queue for those which were working. I'd phoned him to tell him that I'd be late. He told me to wait for him, that he'd come to fetch me. I argued with him, actually, tried to convince him it wasn't necessary, that I wasn't a baby anymore. That I'd be able to come back on my own. That probably Farid and I could walk back together. But he got angry, said I was talking like a fool, being reckless, as always. That it wasn't safe for a young boy, or even two young boys to be roaming around in the dark. Of course, as it turned out, he was in as much danger – more maybe. Maybe, maybe they wanted a man, not a boy! Maybe if he hadn't come for me, we would have got home safely. And then none of this would have happened. None of it would have happened and we'd be home, not here. Maybe … maybe …'

I couldn't help it. I was crying again. So wrapped up in the fabric of make-believe that it became real, even to my own ears, my lying heart. I could almost see it. Men coming behind him, dressed in nightblack clothes to merge into the gloom of the late evening. Hands grabbing him, his arms, hands shooting out to stop his shouting mouth. His struggle, futile, his hopes crashing, his fear for us as much as the fear for himself. In my mind's eye, I am seeing him as I was that night when I had followed him. When he had grabbed me to stop me from screaming out. He has become me of that night. But I was being saved, Abba was being taken. Away. Come back. Come back.

'Here, drink, this, it will make you feel better,' my companion from the other room urges a glass of Fanta to my lips, trying to stem my tears with more liquid. But as I look up, I see only the impatience of the person across the table. He needs to get on, finish with me. There are others, too many others, in the grief-heavy queue. There's no time for my tears. He clears his throat, impatient, 'Carry on.' It is an order, not a request.

'Then, nothing. We waited and waited. We went around all over Srinagar. Markets, lakes, parks. Crowded places, deserted places. But he just disappeared. We hoped and prayed he was safe, alive. Then we started to pray and hope we'd get a ransom note, a call asking for money in exchange for our Abbu. But ... nothing ...'

It was the best I could do. I didn't know if it was enough, but I couldn't do anything else. I gulped some of the sweet orange drink. And waited.

'So, he just disappeared?' The two men exchanged the same look they had earlier. It wasn't a very reassuring one. Something about their look said 'too bad'. I waited – what else could I do?

She shifts nervously in her chair. She's never been comfortable talking to strangers. She has never been at ease talking about her personal life to anyone. And now, she's going to have to do both. She's fighting for the lives of her two sons here. So she swallows her shame and discomfort and squares herself to meet the questions of the hijab-covered woman who examines the file. The sheet that contains all that is left of her life.

'So, Amina begum, it has now been ... how long?'

'Three months,' she doesn't need to ask 'how long since what?' she knows. There's only one question left now.

'Hmmm, now Amina bi, can you tell me the details of what happened? Please give every single detail. The more you can tell us, the more it will help us help you.'

Her mind races, reels, she falters, 'Well, it was such a while ago, I don't know exactly how much I remember ...'

47

'Umer and I should have gone over this. We should have got our story sorted out,' she thinks. Then, it hits her, this *is* an interrogation, Umer was right. That's why they only asked the straight, simple questions earlier, when Umer and she were together. And they insisted on separate questioning for the answers that really mattered. Those that would make or break their case. But they were so wrapped up in their own shame and misery. Unable to talk about what was happening to them. They were so used to skirting around important issues, they had not anticipated this. This questioning – interrogation. And now it was too late. Too late.

The woman across the table continues to wait for the story to unfold. Her impatience manifests in the tapping of her pen against the blank paper before her. She wants to put the facts down and get on to the next sorry tale. Then she wants to go home. Her son's not too well today, a stomach-ache kept him away from school. She wants to be away from all this misery and sorrow. It's beginning to eat into her. She wishes she had a better, happier job. But she's grateful for the job, of course. It has kept her family together and going. Ever since that fateful night when her husband was dragged from their home. She screaming after him, after them. As they stuffed him like a sack into the boot of their car and drove away. She, running after him across the early snow, barefoot, hair coming undone. The frantic search ending in his body being flung outside the gate two days later. She shakes herself out of the awful memories that won't go away, won't even begin to fade. She must stop this. Stop it. There's no good to be gained from re-living those memories every time she has to confront these women. Women too much like her. The same story to tell. She blocks it out. Focuses on her little stomach-achey boy at home and clears her throat impatiently. This is someone else's story, not her's.

'Amina bi, please, I don't have all day, there are many others waiting their turn. What are the circumstances of your husband's er…?' She can't bring herself to say it.

So the mother starts off, wondering if, by some stroke of good luck, her son is spinning the same yarn, telling the same lies. For she is no good at lying.

'Actually, it was getting near to curfew time and I had just discovered I'd run out of milk for the children's breakfast next morning. It was stupid, I'm usually quite careful of these things, especially nowadays. But that day, oh, I don't now, it just slipped my attention. I really should have just kept quiet. The children could have had tea in the morning, what would have been the harm? But I muttered out aloud and my husband overheard me. "No milk for the children?" he asked. He was very particular they ate well. He'd often chide them if they wanted expensive shoes or jeans, but he never skimped over their nourishment. I tried to dissuade him from going out. It was already late. I told him that I'd have the milk for them and make them drink it when they came home from school. But no, it had to be there for their breakfast, he insisted. Then I told him that I'd go. I tried to persuade him it was safer for a woman to be out on the roads in the darkening evening than for a man. Even Umer who heard us, started insisting his Abbu should stay home, that he could go out himself. But my husband would have none of it. He was very protective of me. Never wanted me to tire myself. And definitely, there was no way that we would let Umer go out.'

The woman across the table smiled a warm smile. She felt she knew this man, she felt, she felt she was this woman and she was talking about her life, her husband.

Amina smiled back, feeling more confident now.

'So, he left to get the milk. The boys wanted to go with him, especially Umer who said he needed a new pen for his approaching exams, but his father insisted on going alone. He was always worried for his son's safety. So he left, telling me to get dinner heated and kept ready. "I'll be back in five minutes and I'm hungry …" were the last words we ever heard him say. He never came back.'

'Come back,' her heart cries out, 'come back, my love … It's all my fault,' she weeps out loud, 'it's my fault. If only I'd got the milk. If only … he was hungry and I couldn't even give him one last meal …'

She is crying now, quietly, tears escaping from her soaked handkerchief and spreading dark patches on her lap. She can't help it. She can almost see the hands reaching out to grab at her husband as he strides towards the shops. Hands shooting out to stifle the scream before it escapes. His struggles futile, his hopes crashing. The fantasy more real, sweeter, almost. Then bitter reality.

The ensuing silence is broken again by the tapping pen. 'And then?'

'And then nothing. We waited and waited. For some note, word, sign. But we're still waiting. There's been no indication about who kidnapped him, or what has happened.'

It was the best she could do. The effort of lying has exhausted her. She runs out of words now. She hopes that those she's already spoken are enough. So she waits.

'So, he's just disappeared?' the woman asks, disapproval colouring her voice, twisting her mouth downwards. Ammi is distressed to see the small tell-tale shake of the head. She holds her breath. And waits. What else can she do?

Half

The stories woven by mother and son did not match. How could they? As they stepped out of the Aman office, they exchanged their stories and were horrified, realizing at how divergent they were.

'They'll know we're lying, Ammi. They will know something's wrong.'

'What will they do about it, though, I wonder.'

Both of them left their thoughts, their dread that they had reached a dead end unsaid. The little flame of hope sputtered out before their eyes, extinguished by necessary lies. The slip of paper that they received by post some days later, confirmed their worst fears.

*Granted/***Rejected***

On grounds of unconfirmed circumstance of disappearance.

So that was it, there was going to be no aid. Khalla said we should appeal, try to meet the top man, explain. She said that she would pull the necessary strings. So she got us the appointment with the top man.

He was kind, actually. The first person who listened to us, really listened. He was sympathetic too. He said 'I understand, I'm sympathetic too. But …'

The terrible but – the full stop of hope.

'But ma'am your story about the disappearance of your husband does not match your son's story about his father's disappearance. There are too many discrepancies.'

'But what does past circumstance matter, sir? The fact is my husband has disappeared. The fact remains he was our only breadwinner. That we are living a life of penury is a fact. That my sons may have to drop out of the school, if we can't find money for their fees, their books, their uniforms. This is not changed by this story or that. The fact, sir, is I am a widow, my sons are fatherless – orphaned.'

Ammi's eyes and voice were ablaze with a mixture of rage and desperation. There. She'd said it, we were widow and orphans. If this didn't change this man's mind, then nothing could, or would.

The man nodded slowly, looking carefully at his hands. I looked at them too. Those hands held a lot of power. They held our future, our lives. Ammi, I knew held her breath, was holding it. She too took his slow nod as a yes. The official continued looking at his hands. As though he was reading something there. But you can't read another person's future in the lines of your own palm.

'Half,' he finally said, softly, sadly, 'half.'

We waited. We didn't know what he meant.

'You're not a widow, ma'am, but a half-widow, and your sons are half-orphans.'

'What?' Ammi almost yelped as though she'd been hit. 'What? Because I'm alive, not dead or disappeared myself, my children must suffer? Are you saying that they'd be better off if I was dead?'

'Ammi!' I jumped up and held her, 'Ammi, don't.'

'Not exactly, no ma'am. It's like this ...' finally, he looked up from his hands, he'd read enough. But he still didn't look us in the eye.

'There are many men, good men, who've disappeared because they've been abducted. But there are an equal number of men who've disappeared because they've gone across the border for training, or have joined one or the other of these terrorist outfits that have infested our homes, our land – like termites. They've left their families knowingly. Hoping that organizations like Aman will look after their families for them.'

'But ...,' we both began. He put his hands up in a gesture that implied both helplessness and a request for patience. 'I know, I'm not saying your husband is one of the latter, but, but if there's a – doubt – a chance he has gone to the other side, then ... then we are not authorized. You see, then you are declared "half-widow, half-orphans". I know that your suffering is no less than that of someone whose husband is killed by militants, but, my hands are tied, its policy ... I'm sorry.'

You could tell he was really sorry, but we didn't need pity, we needed money. So we stood, empty-handed, done in by policy. We were halves – not eligible for help, aid, because Abbu had disappeared to the wrong side. The official didn't know if there was anyone, any other organization that could help, would help.

I looked over at my mother and was startled at how old

she suddenly looked. I hadn't seen her ageing. Maybe I hadn't looked. Maybe I don't want to.

And suddenly the fight just left me. I felt old and weary myself. I just wanted someone to take over, take care of me, of us. Take care of things. I just didn't have the energy left for worry any more. Without talking about it, we both walked towards the pavement and sat there, sinking down because our legs wouldn't bear our burden any more. Heads sinking on to our knees because they couldn't bear the weight of our sorrows any longer. We had no energy to try and pep the other person up. No words of hope and comfort. We both knew what this now meant. Despite Ammi's back breaking efforts, there wasn't going to be enough money to see us through the next few years. We knew then, school wasn't to be an option for me any more. I would have to leave to get a job. There simply wasn't enough to pay the fees for both of us. I was being forced to take another unwilling step towards an adulthood I wasn't ready to meet just yet. No matter how much I hated school, no matter how many times I'd wished I didn't have to go. I knew I didn't want to leave it forever. Not yet. At least, I didn't want to be forced into it.

And Ammi, Ammi who'd fought so valiantly, worked so hard to prevent this from happening, now felt defeated and depleted. It was an unfair fight thrust upon her. We sat, each thinking about the other, each unable to find the energy, the fight, the sympathy to put an arm around the other's shoulder, to give sahaaraa, to let the other know they weren't alone.

We are the weeds. The wild, unwanted things. Who wants weeds? No one. Thrown out. Out of everyone's lives. Out of our own lives. I can't help sinking into the sticky mess of self-pity and hopelessness. I can't help it. There doesn't seem to be anything else to do.

A flicker of light

And just when all hope seems to be lost, gone. Forever. Just as the dark tunnel that is life seems seamless and endlessly dark, a chink of light appears. Small, but startlingly bright. So bright you could become, blind.

That night, as we sat, eating our dinner, there was a knock on the door. Small and stealthy. At first, so small that it seemed muffled by the night and fear. At first, we didn't respond. We sat there, frozen, hoping it was just a mouse, cold in the dark. But it came again. Umed's hand, half way up, his mouth open to receive the food, now open in fear. Ammi's hands, instinctively reaching for her sons'. Me, just frozen into dread. A tableau of fear, for a night time knock is rarely a good thing in these violent, torn times.

The knock comes again, a little firmer now, less like the scuffling of a rat sound. A 'open the door quickly' knock. I stand, starting towards the door, but Ammi's hand reaches for me. She clutches at my pyjama, with food-stained hands. 'Oofo, Ammi, now look what you've done,' wiping the rice and gravy from my pyjama, I stride towards the door as another knock, more urgent, more insistent stirs the air in the house. I peep through a chink in the curtains. I can't make out anything. Then suddenly, I shriek, for there are eyes inches away from mine on the other side of the glass pane. Ammi rushes up to me, propelled by a shriek of her own. I turn to instruct Umed, but he's already crawling under the bed. Fear is a good teacher. We don't know who is out there. It can't be good. It can't be, but we have to open the door.

'Who is it?' I whisper, my voice hoarse with fear.

'For God's sake, open the door.'

'First identify yourself.'

'Your Abbu has sent me. I have news.'

Even as Ammi hesitates, even as she's trying to push me forward and hold me back, I open the door and almost pull the man in and shut the door behind him, bolting it.

Ammi waits by the door as I lead him in. I indicate to her with my eyes and head this man is our guest, sent by Abbu. A messenger. We should make him feel welcome. But, instead, she clutches on to the handle of the door. I don't know what she's doing that for. Is she getting ready to throw him out, or bolt, leaving us here with him? The wild animal in her eyes could lead her anywhere.

'Ammi?' I whisper, but she is beyond me now, so I show our 'guest' a chair to sit on. My scalp tingles with anticipation. Is he the bearer of good tidings? Or not? A great apprehension begins to grow inside me. Suppose he's come to tell us Abbu's dead? Suppose Abbu's been killed … ? The fear begins to grow inside me like a live thing. As though my stomach was turning inside out and was coming up through my throat, choking me.

'What?' the choking fear makes my voice high, my question, sharp. What?

'Your Abbu sends his good wishes ...'

'Yah Allah!' Ammi's voice is choked with fear too. Maybe she had the same thought.

'He's, he's all right?'

'Yes, he is – he sends his good wishes ...'

'And?'

'And he hopes you three, his family, are all right. He prays for you everyday.' 'We don't want his prayers.' Ammi is talking, almost to herself.

'Ji?' she spoke so softly the man didn't understand. He looked nervously at her, then back at me. I waited; we both did, waited for the other to find a path through the thorns of this awkward, unexpected meeting. Neither of us could. At least he should have been more prepared.

And that's when I took a good look at him. And found that he wasn't really a man at all! He was a young boy, maybe just about my age. Maybe even younger. He seemed more nervous than I. But, but what was I to say? I couldn't find the words, any words in the parched desert of my throat.

Over the terrain of our awkwardness, then, came a tiny moan. It was Umed, from under the bed. 'When will he come back home?' he asked in a voice much younger than his own.

'He, he says he will try to come, er ... oh ... sometime ...'

'When?'

'I – I don't know. I ...' A whimper from under the bed.

'Why are you here?' Ammi's voice and eyes were narrowed,

57

tight. Contempt edging her bearing. It didn't make it easier for our guest. He looked from Umed, under the bed, to me, to Ammi's feet. He didn't dare look her in the eye.

'Ammi jaan ...,' he started, turning, still seated, towards her. His head bowed low.

'Don't!' she hissed, holding her hand up to stop him, 'don't call me Ammi jaan. Don't try to get into my heart, there's no space for you here or here or here,' she spat, stabbing with her finger at her heart, her head, her home.

'Ammi,' Umed and I pleaded for her to be still. Her rage was a frightening thing. Besides, she had always instilled in us the lesson that you had to look after your guests with due respect, whether you liked them or not. Whether you like them or not. Yet, here she was ...

'Tell me why you are here. Get it over with and then get out.' She commanded, hand still on the doorknob. But now I knew that she wasn't the one who'd leave, I knew for certain now. She wanted him to stop defiling her house as soon as possible.

'M-m-m-ma'am h-he asked m-m-me to find out h-how y-you all are.'

'We're penniless. Tell him that. Tell him. Tell him his wife works as a servant in people's houses. Tell him his elder son will soon drop out of school because we can no longer afford to have him there. Tell him Umer will take up a job now so we can put food in our bellies. You tell him all that. Now go!' She was about to open the door to aid his exit. But he stood, fumbling in his phiran.

'M-ma'am, ma'am, wait. He, he knows, he understands the difficulties and hardships you must be enduring. He is a great man. He is like a father to me. He's a very kind man, that's why, that's why he wanted you to have, to have … this.' He held out a zipped up pouch, stretching his arm out towards her with a trembling hand. But she looked at it with such contempt, her mouth downturning in such disgust, as though it were a dead pig in the boy's hand, that he turned and held it out to me instead. His eyes pleading, 'take it, please take it …'

But looking at Ammi, I wasn't sure I should. Suddenly, Umed darted out from his hiding place and snatched at the pouch, unzipping it greedily.

'Abbu sent it? For us? Is there something for me? Is it something to eat?' As the pouch opened, money cascaded from Umed's hands and fluttered on to the floor like butterflies. Five hundred rupee notes, some pink notes I didn't even recognize. Money. More money than we'd seen in a long, long time. In fact, more money than I'd ever seen in my entire life. Put together. Umed's face lit up, his long dark eyelashes fluttering like butterflies themselves. He fell to his knees, sweeping up the money into his arms, his expression saying, 'Saved! We are saved at last!'

'Don't touch it. Leave it.' Ammi commanded furiously. Umed looked at her surprised, confused. What was she saying?

'Umed, I said leave it. Step away from that filth.'

'Ammi,' he began earnestly, smiling, almost, believing she hadn't understood what this was and what it meant. 'Ammi, this isn't filth, Ammi, it's money. Abbu sent money. He knows we need it. See, that's why he had to go away, to make our lives better, more comfortable. See how much money Abbu's sent for us, Ammi.'

Looking passionately, earnestly into her face, hoping to sway her by the sheer speed and volume of his words. 'Ammi, see, now you can relax, you don't have to work. Why, you can even have a servant of your own now,' he was bubbling, giggling, in his excitement. Desperate, because he could see from her face that her heart was stone. 'And, and Ammi, just think. Umer bhai doesn't have to leave school now. He can study. He can even go to college. Ammi, please, Ammi …,' but the enthusiasm was ebbing out of him, his voice faltering. Ammi hadn't backed off at all. Not softened at all.

'Umed, you heard me. Get up off the floor and leave that garbage. And you …,' she said, turning to the boy who'd brought the money. 'You, pick that up, take it back from where you came and tell your boss, or whatever he is to you, we don't need his dirty money. We don't need his charity. We're managing perfectly well without him.'

'But Ammi…' Umed tried one last time, still sitting, crouched near the money, unable to wrench himself away from it.

'Umed,' suddenly Ammi roared, making the three of us flinch, jump. 'Get away from that money.'

Umed, without even the will to stand on his feet, crawled away and back under the bed. Like a whipped dog, whimpering.

The boy stood uncertainly, looking at the floor. He'd got one set of clear instructions that seemed simple enough when he got them. He was to have been the harbinger of good news, the bearer of succor, good tidings and relief. He was told that he'd be received with open arms, and, who knows, even be given some mother-cooked food. As a reward. Yes, yes, he was warned the mother could be a bit fiery, but that her heart would melt once he'd called her Ammi and shown her all the money. He had been looking forward to meeting Abbu's sons about whom he talked often. He had begun to think of them as his own brothers, bound together by the strength of his mentor's arms.

But here, it was all gone wrong. The woman who seemed quite small and fragile when he'd entered, now, seemed to have grown physically before his very eyes, till she towered above him and threatened to reduce him to ash. And the money? What should he do with all this money? How could he bear to go back to his mentor, his Abbu, as he called him now, and confess he'd failed in his mission? His very first mission he'd earned for being so diligent and obedient. A simple mission that now lay scattered on the floor, in ruins.

He looked up again. This time with the glaze of tears glittering in his eyes. His chin wobbled a bit, 'just like Umed's', thought Umer. The boy looked up with pleading eyes, 'Ammi jaan, please, y-you're just like my Ammi …'

'Then why aren't you home with her?' Ammi's question was still harsh, but, you could tell her tone was gentler. The wobbly chin must have done it. It looked so much like Umed's when he was about to cry.

'Son, go home, go back to your own Ammi, she must be worried sick for you. You don't need to do this. It's – it's not good. This is not good.' Her hand swept to take in all the scattered money.

Suddenly, as if the burden of the truth of her words was too much to bear, the boy sank to the ground, right on to the ruins of his mission. His head bowed so low that his chin rested on his chest. Ammi's hand went to her mouth. She was able to fight, and shout and throw the boy out of the house. But she wasn't prepared for this.

'Son, son don't do this – you don't have to do this.' I didn't know whether she meant his working with Abbu, or just simply his sitting there on the floor, so sunk with sorrow. Just as suddenly, the boy started to cry, great heaving sobs shaking his frame. Umed shot out from under the bed and ran to put an arm around him. Giving vent to tears of his own.

Ammi told me to get water for the boy. When I got back, I found Umed gathering up the money and stuffing it back into the pouch. Ammi kneeling on the ground, her hand on the boy's shoulder. My heart leapt. At last, she'd relented. She was going to accept the money. Our problems were over, perhaps.

'Son, I don't know how you got mixed up in all this, but it is wrong. And I'm happy to see that you now know it's wrong too. Just walk away. Walk away, it's not too late. Take the money back …'

The three of us boys each started at this, 'Ammi.'

'Umer, Umed, we're not going to accept this money. I made that clear to your father before he left. And I'm making it clear to you. I don't care what the cost is; what we have to do, or do without, we're not touching blood money. Is that clear?' She looked at me.

'Yes, Ammi.'

'Is that clear?' the question was directed to Umed. He looked back at her. His eyes didn't agree, but his voice didn't have the himmat, the courage, to disagree.

'Umed, is it clear? You touch this money, you try to use even one rupee and I'll throw you out of this house. Don't think I won't. I threw your father out; I'll do the same to you. Do you understand me? Umed?'

'Yes, Ammi jaan.'

The last of the notes went into the pouch and Umed zipped it up to show that he had actually understood. She shifted her gaze to our guest; her tone was softer with him than it was with us. 'Do you understand?' He nodded, his head still hanging. She put her hand back on his shoulder. 'Have you eaten, are you hungry?'

The boy had hoped to have a meal cooked by a mother's hand. He'd only eaten half of his ration before setting off, in anticipation of it. He nodded again. This time his chin left his chest and he allowed himself the faintest smile. She smiled back at him too.

'Umer,' she said, 'go and see if there's a little food left over. There won't be much, but bring what ever there is.'

When I went, I found our plates still had food on them. Especially Ammi's, she'd hardly eaten. There was some left in the pots. Not much, as Ammi knew, but some. I doled it out, feeling suddenly resentful. When he first came, I was awkward she was not treating him like one should a guest. But now that she was being all soft with him, offering him food that wasn't even enough for us, I felt angry and resentful and wanted her to send him away, back into the night. I thought of the money too. I didn't agree with her about not keeping it. I didn't know why she was being so stubborn. Why couldn't she ask *us* what *we* wanted? But I didn't have the courage to confront her just now. So I picked up her plate as well and brought the two plates in.

The boy was washing his hands, Umed was helping him. They smiled at each other, warmly, like friends, like brothers. I felt a stab of jealously. We hadn't smiled like that at each other for a long time.

'Ammi, you finish your food too,' I said.

'Yes, yes and get your plate and your brother's. We'll eat together now,' she said.

63

Once we'd settled down, like a family, Ammi picked up the threads that had hung loose since the boy collapsed on to the floor. The pouch, I saw, was on the little table near the door, ready for its departure.

'What's your name, son?'

Oh so now we had to share both our parents with this boy?

'Hameed ...'

His story unravelled under Ammi's probing. He was from Sopore. His father was a mason, doing quite well as there were plenty of people adding floors to their usual single storied houses. He was contracted by a Fidayeen group for some masonry work; to rebuild an old house abandoned by some Kashmiri Pandit family. First he helped them with just the building, then, he helped them out financially, when some money they were expecting was late in arriving. Then, slowly, he began to take an active part in the group's workings. Hameed's mother didn't like it. She felt he should be safe – 'what will we do if something happens to you?' was a favourite refrain.

The three of us looked at each other; we'd heard that line in our family too. It was as if he was telling us our story!

Then, one night, there was a 'job' to be carried out. The army supply trucks were headed for the higher reaches of the snow-bound mountains. They were to be blown up in a Fidayeen attack.

'What's Fidayeen?' asked Umed. Ammi and I looked at each other. Should we tell him? Should a child this young know about suicide bombers who kill themselves in a desperate attempt to kill others? But Hameed was already explaining about the Fidayeen. Bombers who don't set off their explosives by remote control or a timer, they actually strap the bombs on to themselves. They know, as they do it, that it'll be one of the last things they do.

They blow themselves up in the attack. Umed's eyes were round with surprise and horror. I could see the flickering question 'WHY?' in his face. But he didn't interrupt as Hameed went on to tell how the man who was to carry out the attack had run away, just disappeared at the last moment. It was Hameed's father who'd volunteered and martyred himself.

Umed was about to ask what martyred meant, but the gasp of horror from Ammi was explanation enough.

'Well, people from his group, his commander, came to tell us and give us a final letter and some of his personal belongings. And in the letter, there was a request, a last wish, to see one of his sons, at least, to follow in his footsteps.

Ah! Those blighted footsteps again. Aren't sons expected to follow in their father's footsteps – no matter where those footsteps lead?

'And your Ammi – she, she let you?' Ammi's voice couldn't rise beyond a disbelieving whisper. And he could only whisper back his reply.

'No.'

'No?'

'No, no, she didn't; she would never let me, any one of us.'

'Then?'

'She, she fainted when she heard the commander read out this part of the letter. She passed out. And the man took me by the hand and led me out of the house.'

'And you let him?'

'It was my father's last wish.'

So he'd left his fainted mother and followed those footsteps that had led to his father's death. And he'd never been back home after that.

65

Thick silence filled the room. There was hardly more to say. The food was still uneaten. We sat there – oh, maybe an hour, a day, two minutes. Who knows? But the images that floated up for each of us, filled us, were finally, broken by the chirping of birds and the cocks crowing. It was morning.

On the brink of a very hard truth

He looked towards the window, a gasp escaping his lips, 'Oh no!'

'It's all right,' whispered Ammi, 'Hameed, it's all right.'

'No, no,' he scrambled up, panicking, to his feet. 'No, no, I should have been back. I was supposed to reach home right away. At night, itself …'

'Where you came from, Hameed. Last night, where you came from, that's not your home. Don't mistake it for home, don't call it home.'

'Yes, but …'

'Sit down. Stay. You can't leave now, not in the day. We'll give you shelter for now. Leave when it is dark, tonight.'

He slumped, nodding, against the door, knowing that she was right. The sunlight was his enemy. He would have to stay here.

'Abbu will be so worried …,' he whispered.

'But I thought your Abbu was …,' began Umed, wondering whether he had misunderstood.

'He calls our Abbu, Abbu, Umed.'

'Why?'

'Because he's such a good man. A great man. He's like my own Abbu. That's why …'

'Ammi, Ammi, why does he get to live with our Abbu and not me? Why can't I go with Hameed and be with Abbu for some time?'

I thought she was going to slap him. The way her arm rose, fist clenched. But she brought that fist up to her mouth and bit into her fingers. She snapped her eyes shut, but not before some tears were able to escape and glisten on the tired corners of her eyelids.

'Yah, Allah,' she moaned. Umed looked stricken, torn between the pain of her reaction and his longing for his Abbu.

'You see,' she said, turning to Hameed who still stood by the door. By the money. 'You see how it is. Little boys like him will go off in search of their fathers. And find death instead.'

'But I wouldn't die, Ammi, I'd live with him, because he's my Abbu. He won't let anything bad happen to me.'

'He left you, Umed. Don't you understand? He's left you because being your Abbu was not good enough for him any more. Or at least, not enough. No, he had to go and fight a battle that wasn't his to fight. A battle where there will be no winners, only losers. A battle, in fact, with no end.'

'But…'

'No, there's no argument.'

'Ammi, Hameed has him as his father, then why can't I? Why can't I? I'm his son, his real son. Ammi, please Ammi, how can you be so cruel?'

She turned to me then, defeated. But I had no words, so I looked at Hameed, surprised to find him crying, trying not to, but crying. There were too many tears that morning. And no answers.

'All right,' said Ammi, 'all right. Umed, you want to go to your father – go.'

'Ammi, no!' I cried, shocked. I knew how against this she was.

'Yes, Umer. If his heart is set on it, then who am I to stop him?'

'You're his mother.'

We looked over at Hameed as he spoke. So solemnly. 'You're his Ammi, that's why you should stop him.'

'But you didn't stop,' whined Umed, peeved, seeing this glimmer of a chance slipping away.

'No, I didn't. But she would have stopped me if she could. If her body hadn't failed her then, at the moment of my leaving.'

'And do you wish she had?' I couldn't help but ask. I had to know.

'No,' he said, surely.

Then immediately after: 'I – I don't know,' there was less surety in his voice now.

'Sometimes …,' he admitted, looking over to Ammi, as if seeking forgiveness, or understanding from his own. She took his hand in both her own. But looked over at Umed, pinning him with the directness of her gaze.

'Look, Umed, we must all take our own decisions. I have tried to make your decisions for you. I have tried to make you see things my way. But, obviously, I have failed. Maybe, maybe, your father is right. Maybe it's me who is wrong, so I should be the one to step out of your path. But, no matter what, no matter what the rights and wrongs, I cannot, now or ever, accept violence as a road. Fighting and killing may be the right way – but they are not my way. This will never be my way.'

We were looking at her, trying to see the end of her long speech. Ammi was never given to long speeches. I'd certainly never heard one like this before. But she wasn't finished.

'But I see today, that I cannot take this decision for anyone else. So Umed, and you too, Umer, if you feel that your future lies with your Abbu and that is the life you want, then I won't stop you. Tonight itself, you can leave with Hameed and go to your Abbu, if that is what you're sure you want.'

'Ammi!' cheerily, brightening up, Umed threw his arms around her, 'Shukriya Ammi jaan. Thank you, thank you.'

'You want to go so much?' Ammi's voice was wistful, her eyes infinitely sad.

'Of course, Ammi.'

'And you, Umer?'

I looked at her, she was losing her son, she'd lost her husband, 'No,' I said, though my heart longed to say yes. 'No. I'll stay here, with Ammi.'

'But I can still go?' he asked again, looking hopefully at her, hardly daring to believe his luck at this change of mind.

'Yes, Umed, you can go.' Her face had hardened, her jaw set, although sadness still clung to her voice and made her fragile shoulders droop. 'Yes, go, if that's what you want. But …'

Her voice, its tone, stopped him as he turned to get his things, 'But it's an irreversible decision. You must choose one of us. If you choose to go, Umed, then you will not come back. Ever.'

'Ever?'

'Yes, Umed. You will never come back to me once you decide to go to your Abbu. You have to know, once you've gone, you've lost me, your home, your school, your friends.'

'Why?' he was horrified, 'Ammi – what are you saying? You're, you're just being mean. Yes, yes, you're mean, that's what you are. Why, Shaukat's father got a job in Saudi Arabia – so far away. Shaukat and his sister went there for their winter holidays. But their Ammi didn't say "you can't come back!"' Even as he mimicked her, he burst into angry tears at the injustice of it all.

And she, she looked so stricken. Hurt beyond belief. In raw pain. She opened her mouth to say something, but a river of grief was choking her. It had to be me. I had to be the one to explain. So I did. The best I could – honestly.

'Umed, sit down.'

'No, no, why should I? It's so unfair, why should I have to choose?'

'Sit down.'

He did, still muttering, shaking his head, glowering resentfully at Ammi. I waited for him to still his fretting. Finally he looked up at me, saw I was waiting. With one final shrug of irritation and a deep breath, he was ready to hear what I had to say to him.

'Umed, my brother. There's something you don't know about Abbu. He hasn't gone to Saudi Arabia for a job like Shaukat's father.'

'Oof ho, as if I don't know that.'

'Then you know what Abbu does?'

He was quiet.

'Fine, then keep quiet and listen, don't interrupt me, hear me out okay? Our Abbu, it's not, it's not an ordinary job he's gone to...'

Dear God, how do you say these things out loud, how do you tell a doting son – your own little brother?

'Umed, you remember that day when we had a big fight on the road?'

'Ya,' said Umed, his anger completely dissolved, his eyes merry with memory. 'You remember how you made a complete ullu out of that fauji man – telling them that our father worked in the chilli fields. He was completely fooled, that man – I was dying to laugh, but I knew that that would spoil it all!

That's what I loved about my boey, he could be so very angry one moment and the next, he could forget it completely, be happy and full of laughter. But this was no time for his childish giggles. He was on the brink of a very hard truth.

'But you know, of course, that I lied about Abbu, don't you?' He nodded, so I went on, 'Did you wonder why I lied – why I *had* to lie about our father?'

He half knew, but he didn't want to.

'Do you remember the thing Salim said about Abbu – that he was a bad man, a jihadi, who almost was caught and was now on the run from the police and the army?'

He nodded, his eyes wide, round.

'Well, Umed, our Abbu is a wanted man. He can never come back. He chose the jihad over us.'

'No, no, you're lying. You're such a bloody liar…'

'Umed look,' I took his face in my hands. He had to understand, I wished he didn't, but he did. 'Dekh, boey, when your friends were told by their parents not to play with you anymore, it was because they knew our Abbu had become an atankvadi. And then, a man on the run from the law. He lives in hiding. He's been responsible, I'm sure, at least partly, for some of the attacks, the bombs and explosions reported in the news ... for some of the deaths.'

'Hameed?' Umed turned to him, in a last ditch attempt at denying the awful, ugly truth. 'They're wrong aren't they?'

'No, Umed, it's the truth,' said Hameed, echoing Ammi's earlier words, 'Your father is a wonderful man, a great man. We don't use the word atankvadi. He is a jihadi, fighting for the good of all of our people, our land and us. But yes, he was almost caught by the fauj and now he is in hiding.'

'That's why, Umed, he can't come back here anymore. That's why he left suddenly at night, knowing he couldn't come back to us anymore. He chose to leave us.'

Umed was silent, for a while, soaking in, absorbing the truth he'd known all along, but denied. We were silent too. These were truths we'd known but never acknowledged, not openly. We'd tiptoed around the facts of Abbu's altered life and never uttered the words out in the open.

'But he still loves us, cares about us. He's worried about us, Ammi, Umer. Look, he sent us so much money.'

'It's blood money, Umed,' said Ammi, 'it's money earned from killing, or from planning to take innocent lives. It will not be used in this house. Not as long as I'm alive.'

'And yet, you're willing to let me go there?'

'No Umed, I'm not willing. I was never willing for your father to go there either. Allah knows I begged, fought with him to leave it. I knew it would be difficult for him to leave, once you're in it, it's hard to get out. So I even suggested we leave Kashmir. Relocate elsewhere, start a new life. But he was in too deep. And he didn't want to leave. And I was too far away from him. Our paths had taken different turns.'

'But, you'll let me go?' you could tell Umed had one foot planted in each of his parent's paths. Wanting her to let him go and begging her to force him to stay.

'I won't stop you, my son. I won't be happy, but if this is what you want, if this is your decision, I will accept.'

'But …'

'But, you will have to accept my decision too. If you choose to join your father, then I cannot take you back.'

'Why?' Umed's voice was a plaintive whine that made Ammi wince.

'Because you're not Shaukat going away to his father for a vacation. Your father has chosen a path from which there is no turning back. And you will be doing the same if you join him. Umed, this is a big decision. One, I think, you shouldn't have to make, young as you are. But circumstance has forced us, the moment is upon us. Take today to think things over. Hameed will only leave at night, under the cover of darkness. If by the evening you decide not to go, then he will leave alone. We will continue our life as we were. I know our lives have been hard since Abbu left. I know you have been very patient, doing without so many things your friends have, but it is our life, our way. And I believe we will find a way out of the hardships too.

'But if you decide you must go to your Abbu, then Hameed will take you there. And you will stay there with him. Remember there will be hardships there as well. This money does not buy luxuries in the life your father leads. I will be sorry to let you go, but I will,' her voice caught, snagged on her tears, 'let you go'.

Umed shifted uncertainly from one foot to another until Ammi told him to go and sit quietly by himself and think about all she had said and the decision he had to make.

'I need tea,' she turned to me, exhausted by the long emotional night, the long speech she'd made, 'we could all do with some.'

I went to the kitchen to make the tea. As I glanced back, I saw Umed open the door and stand there, Hameed wincing as though the clear morning light hurt him. Had he become such a creature of darkness? Was he unable to look at a clear, honest morning anymore? Would Umed too become so? Would I, if I were to go? I wanted to go.

Once again the yearning seized me. I wanted so much to go to Abbu. I knew if Ammi had not put the condition that if we chose to go, there was no coming back, if she hadn't said that, well, for sure, I'd be packing my bags right now, readying to leave with Hameed tonight.

I poured the boiling tea into four glasses and carried them out. Umed sat on the steps. Ammi sat on a chair, Hameed at her feet. They were deep in conversation.

Everything changes

Hameed sat at Ammi's feet. His hands massaging her ankle – her right ankle, exactly where it hurt after she twisted her foot many years ago. How did he know where it hurt her? Her right ankle, not the left one – the right one. How did he know? Had she told him, asked him to massage it, like she often, but not lately, asked Umed and me to? Had she really accepted him so completely that she allowed him to do something so – so, intimate? She didn't even look up when I came into the room with the tea. In fact, she smiled at him, put her hand on his head and stroked his springy head. They were deep in conversation.

I hated him. Then.

I left the tea on the floor next to them. They abruptly stopped talking as I neared. She looked up and smiled. A more benign and peaceful smile than I'd seen on her for the longest time. I couldn't stand it. Why had this stranger, who she hated the sight of, hated for the money he so smugly brought, suddenly found a place in her heart? How had he suddenly made her so serene and peaceful? More than I, her eldest son, was able to these past few months?

I hated him.

I took the remaining glasses of tea and went out to sit with Umed, leaving the door wide open, as though to expose him. But also to try to catch drifts of conversation that escaped through the open door. My attention still veered towards Ammi and Hameed, wondering, wondering what they were suddenly so immersed in. How had they found so much common ground to walk on, where none existed a few hours ago?

Umed took the tea from me. Not complaining that the glass was too hot. He usually yelped when he took his tea or milk, always complaining his fingers were grievously burned. But now, he held the glass as though he had a man's hardened hands. Already.

And when he spoke, it was in a man's voice, a somber man's voice, 'I will go,' he said, 'Bhai, Ammi has told me to sit and think over my decision very carefully. But I don't need time, I've already made up my mind. I'm going.'

'Even if there's no coming back?' my voice sounded younger, peevish, almost. It was as if we had reversed roles. He the older, the wiser, the decision-maker between us, and me the younger, gutless one, and who preferred a life with mother to the adventurous world outside.

'I wish she had not put this condition, but, in a way, I can understand why she has. I can see that for her there is no turning back either. You have to be on one side or the other. I wish she had not, but it doesn't change my decision, my choice. I will go.'

'Doesn't it worry you that your life may be harder than it is here?'

'No.' he said simply, and I saw he really wasn't worried about anything. He had made up his mind and was ready to face the consequences. It had been a simple decision for him after all. Not an easy one, I'm sure, but a straightforward one. His clear choice cast shadows on my own. He seemed to sense this, for he asked, 'What about you, Umer? Will you come too?' Even now, his tone had no childish longing to it. He wasn't begging me to come along with him to make it easier for him; he just wanted to know my thoughts on the matter.

'No,' I said, slowly, reluctantly, 'no, I can't.'

'Why?'

'Who will look after Ammi? We can't leave her alone.'

'And that's your only reason?'

'Yes!' I snapped, as I slammed the door on my cowardice. I saw my uncertainty glimmer behind the truth of my unwillingness to venture into the unknown that lay ahead on Abbu's path. As much as I longed for him, I didn't have the courage to follow him, join him. Perhaps I was relieved by Ammi's terrible condition. It made it justifiable that I must be the responsible son and stay back with her.

'Good,' said Umed, 'that makes it easier for me. Both our parents will have a son each. That's only fair, don't you think?'

'Hmm ...'

'And that stupid Hameed doesn't have to pretend to be Abbu's son, and Abbu doesn't have to pretend that he is, hain na?' Umed's giggle finally sounded like his old chirpy self. The child awake in him at last.

'Yeah, I hate him, don't you?' And we both nodded vigorously and looked in. Ammi and he were looking out at us, smiling. Ammi looked younger and more beautiful than I'd seen her for a long time.

She waved to us and gestured for us to come in. We looked at each other, Umed and I, shrugged and walked back in to find Hameed still massaging Ammi's foot. It was really irritating me now. Although, with a guilty pang I also remembered that neither of us had bothered to massage her for so long. Even when she would ask, we'd start out and then stop quite soon, mostly before she had a chance to tell us we'd done enough, the pain had gone. Okay, I promised myself, this would be one of the things that I'd do after Umed went. I'd massage her feet every evening. She must be in pain with all the work she had to do. I swore to myself that I'd do it, if only this stranger would stop it now. But he didn't, quite oblivious of the fact his actions were making me uncomfortable, he carried right on.

Ammi was beaming as she asked us to sit. She also stroked the back of Hameed's head, whispering, 'Bas beta, that's more than enough.'

'Nahin, Ammi,' he insisted, 'I'm enjoying it so much, please let me.' And she smiled down at him and he at her. With a click of annoyance I was unable to hold back, I sat and Umed sat close to me. Obviously trying to show we were a team, the real brothers, the real sons. Not him. Never him.

'There is some good news,' Ammi said, smiling, relaxed, looking amazingly fresh, although it had been a long, sleepless night.

'Is Abbu coming back?' Umed burst out.

'No, beta, that will never happen now. This is something else.'

We waited; again they exchanged their secret smiles.

'It's about Hameed, he has decided …'

'Ammi convinced me …'

'That he will leave all this …'

'Behind …'

'And he will return …'

'Back to my ammi …'

'Forever,' they both said, together.

'Return?'

'But what about Abbu? What about the others, will they let him go?'

'What about me – how will I go now?'

And between the two of them, they explained to the two of us that Hameed would go back once more. He would take the money back with him with the message that we did not have any need for it – *any need? Of course there was a need – a desperate need.* And he would take Umed with him, if that is what Umed wanted. And then, he would leave the group and make his way back to his home.

'But, but, I thought you said that once you're in it, there's no going back?'

'Yes, yes,' insisted Umed, 'you said yourself and that if I go now I can't come back again – how come you're telling him that he can go back to his house, but you won't let me come back to mine?'

'You are right, Umed, I hadn't thought of that …,' whispered Ammi, which brought a gleam to Umed's eyes.

'So, so, I can go with Hameed and when he leaves, he can bring me back here, that's okay then isn't it, Ammi, we can do that no?'

'No!'

'No?'

'No, Umed, I'm sorry, but no. I will not take you back. Please understand, I cannot.'

'You want his mother to take him back, after he wilfully walked out on her. After he took advantage of the fact that she had fainted. Yet, you can't forgive a little boy, a child, for wanting to meet his own father. You put impossible conditions, you …'

I was so angry with her then. What gave her the right? Who was she to call all the shots, decide what we could do and couldn't do?

She looked at me silently for a bit, considering my words. I thought maybe she was going to change her mind, let him visit Abbu and then come back.

But she was adamant. If either of us went, we could stay gone. She would not have us back.

'So, Umed, is your mind made up, you are leaving for sure?'

'Yes, Ammi, I want to see Abbu. I have so much I want to ask him. I want to see him. He, he never even said goodbye to me.'

She sighed, she was sad, but she didn't soften her stand. She just sat there and shook her head. And then she said, 'I'll be sorry to see you go, my son. For I love you dearly. But I will not stand in your way. If this is your decision, I'll respect it. I don't like it, as I'm sure you don't like mine. But you must respect my decision just as I respect yours. I will let you go and you must.'

It was on the tip of my tongue to tell her that maybe she should be the one to leave. But I couldn't. I don't know how it was that she had convinced Hameed, but he seemed so much at peace. But it was more amazing to see how peaceful she looked – no, not only peaceful, triumphant, almost. She may have convinced a stranger to 'mend his wayward ways', as I'm sure she thought of it. But she was also about to lose her own son. The darling of the household. And on her decision. How could she be peaceful, triumphant?

Ah well, I complain too much. Maybe it's all for the best, who knows? As my grandmother often said, 'God does what is best for us and it is best we don't question Him.' She also said our parents were God's representatives on Earth and so we had to follow them unquestioningly. In any case, my questions weren't yielding any answers, except those I did not want to hear.

And so it was decided. Umed, who was very certain he had made his choice and that choice led him out of our lives, was to accompany Hameed to Abbu's home, outfit, den – what do you call it? Hameed would take the money. All of it. And he would somehow leave – escape from it all. They were not to reveal this plan to anyone, not even to Abbu.

Morning sounds permeated our home. Calling us back into the real, mundane world. And Ammi decided that she must go to work, but that we would stay indoors. There was no need for us to go to school. In any case, Umed was leaving it forever and it was not as if he could go around announcing his farewell. And I, well, now that it was certain I would have to drop out of school and take up a job, I didn't need to go back for any farewells either. Ammi must have been tired, but I didn't feel like being the good son and offering her I could go in her place and do her work so she could rest and spend some last hours with Umed. I didn't feel like, at all, but I did feel guilty as she heaved herself off the chair and made for the toilet. Hameed's look of – what was it, anger? disappointment? – didn't help matters. But I wanted to stay with Umed. I knew Ammi did too. How could she not?

But I was too angry. Too, I don't know – desperate? She was losing her son, but I was losing my brother. I would have taken him back like a shot. I didn't need to think. Even if he strayed on to a criminal's path, I would take him back. He was my brother – what else would I do, what else could I do? How could she not – why would she not?

She came out, ready to set off. She left a little money, telling me to get some bread, some biscuits. Telling me to help Umed pack for his journey, for his departure. 'Make sure he has everything he needs. Give him a good breakfast, give him …,' her voice choked over. She turned away, but not before we saw the tears well up in her eyes.

'Umed …,' she said, turning, beseeching, begging him, without a word, to stay. 'Umed … meri jaan … meri jaan …'

And yes, you could see the life draining out of her as she cut the bonds that tied her to her departing son. He ran to her and she wrapped him in her arms. They wept and I thought again, either she would let him come back, or he would change his mind. I know I would have. I know I was crying too, standing all alone on my island. Hameed too cried. Was it for us or for what he himself had resolved to leave behind?

But no one changed their minds. I seemed to be the only one standing on shifting sands. After they cried their tears and murmured their apologies to each other, Ammi kissed Umed's forehead and blessed him and wished him Godspeed and happiness and begged him to be careful. Then she turned to Hameed and said, 'All right, my son, this is it, this is goodbye. You must be gone by six in the evening. Umer will make some dinner for you, eat and then leave. You must not leave any later.' She was right, of course. Moving about in the absolute dark here in the city, especially two boys, one so inexperienced and the other just a boy, was not a good idea.

And so it was done. And she was gone. Never to see her younger son. Again.

After the leaving

The walls closed in on us, on me, after Umed left. There was now a fear in Ammi, a desperation I too would vanish one day. She watched me closely, all the time, every moment we were together. And even sometimes when we weren't, it seemed her eyes were on me, the leash pulled taut, the invisible collar she had put around my neck tightening, choking me. She got me a job in a cloth shop just near the house. I was a shop assistant; never meeting, interacting with customers, just folding bales of cloth, the dupattas unfurled like masts of a ship that would never sail. I was fed at the shop and given wages. She dropped me to the shop in the morning, on her way to work and she picked me up on her way back. I was not to step out on my own at all. The little jobs I used to do before, I was no longer allowed. Even just getting the milk, the bread was no longer on the cards for me. She did it on her way home. I was amazed none of my friends came over to our house to enquire why I was no longer coming to school. It was as if I had become invisible, ceased to exist. Only a pair of hands folding cloth, sweeping and dusting. Nothing more. Maybe less.

Our lives were mundane, the routine unchanging. The taste of our food unaltered. We lived from day to day, having dispensed even with conversation, doing nothing beyond the necessary, 'How was your day?' 'All right, and yours?' kind of exchange, meaningless but obligatory. Nothing more. Maybe less. Often, not even this much.

Sometimes, in the quiet of the morning, I would whisper my name to myself, just to hear it. Just to confirm I was there, present, alive. When I was alone, in the long evenings of the fast approaching winter, in the long nights when morning seemed an impossible dream and sleep would not come, I'd wish she were with me, yearn for her, long for her to come and talk to me.

But when she was with me, every moment of my few moments outside, I wished I was alone. That she'd leave me alone. But she never did. I was never alone outside. Never to be trusted, paying for the sins of those who left her. Although I was the only one who hadn't.

Homecoming

As one day bleed seamlessly into the next featureless one, we sleepwalked through our lives. Barely doing anything extra, barely eating the extra mouthful, barely looking out at the first snowflake that melted before it had even settled, barely breathing. Hardly existing.

Then

One day.

A screech of brakes, a shout. Other voices gasping, screaming. Doors slamming, children pulled inside. A car, truck, jeep, whatever it was, arriving on screeching, protesting tyres.

Then

Silence.

A stillness that was dreadful. Deathly. For there was death.

We crept to the window, peeping out fearfully. What did the screeching and screaming mean? Where did the silence lead?

We crept to the window, peering out. Dreading what we might see. For perhaps we knew what we were going to see. And we saw it. The body. Broken and bleeding. The red pinking the snow. The body unmistakable. It was too well-known. Too well loved. By us. Me.

Abbu.

The face already white. The body too broken for repair. He lay there. He had come home at last. But what a homecoming. What a reunion. Ammi was holding me, in a grip that was tight and fierce. Or was it frightened? We were glued to the window, unmindful of other faces looking at him. At us. They were waiting for us to make the first move. But we didn't know what move to make. We were paralysed. Until Ammi, as yet dry-eyed, turned to me with horror on her face and whispered, 'Umed!'

The word, the name galvanized us into action. We rushed out to the body of the man who'd already left us long before he died. Ammi rushed to him shouting, 'Umed, where is my Umed, where is my son?' she shouted down at Abbu's snowcold, snowpale face. She shook him by his frozen shoulders, as though her frenzy could wake him for just a moment to reveal where our Umed was. But there were no answers. Only questions, those hovering questions. Unceasing.

'Ammi,' I shook her, as gently as I could, although I wasn't feeling gentle. 'Ammi, let's take him inside.'

'But where's my Umed?'

'We'll find out, Ammi, we'll look for him, but we can't stay out here. Let's take him inside.'

'Where?'

'Home. Abbu's come home to you, Ammi, let's take him in.'

'But …'

'People are staring Ammi, we have to go in.'

That's when we looked up, responding to the sound of footsteps crunching the snow. The boots were unmistakable. Abbu had been brought home by the army. They had found him at last.

We carried him. Our neighbours watching, not one coming forward to help. Only looking through windows or even out in the open. Shaking their disapproving heads, thankful they weren't us. We carried him. Struggling, because now there were only two of us. I didn't want their help, the army's help. I didn't want them to touch him. Anymore. So we struggled, carrying him between the two of us. And although she was quite strong, she was also tiny and frail.

We carried him. Back towards the house he had been banished from, from where he had banished himself. Struggling to keep the door open while we carried him in was futile. We had to put him down on the verandah where he had sat me down to talk to me just before he left. He lay there now. Beyond words of advice or apology. One of the officers came forward, holding the door open for us. He had his head down, his army hat blocking his eyes. We picked Abbu's body up again. He was stiff and heavy. But we carried him and laid him on the ground.

And then we looked at each other, we didn't know what to do with him, to him. What now? We asked each other, though we didn't say a word. The question of Umed was the only thing that kept us alive. Together. The army people stood outside. We could feel their presence more than hear the scraping of their boots. They gave us a few precious moments before they knocked on the door and then walked in, without waiting for an answer.

One of them, the one in charge probably, put his hand on my shoulder as I hunched over Abbu. He left his hand there for a moment, doing nothing, just letting his presence be felt, before he increased the pressure slightly, squeezed my shoulder, to indicate he wanted more than to deliver Abbu's body and watch us hunkered dry-eyed over him. I tried to ignore it, but I knew and he knew I was just playing for time.

I turned, looked at him, and then stood. Ammi didn't react at all. She seemed to be in a world of her own. Gone wherever Abbu was now. I turned and looked at him then. The man had a kind face, he had taken off his army cap and looked more like a normal person. He indicated I should go outside with him where we could talk.

We stood just where Abbu and I had been when he bade me his last goodbyes. We stood there now and the army man looked at me. I was waiting for him to make the first move, ask the first question.

'Did you know that your father was involved in the militant violence?'

What should I have answered? I knew, of course I knew, but was I to concede that I did, or feign ignorance? I looked at him blankly, at least I hope it was blankly, but he looked carefully at my face, into my eyes, as though reading it, looking for the answer that wouldn't come out of my mouth. Maybe he found it, for he nodded. He'd understood. That I knew, we knew.

'We have not killed your father,' he said, putting his hand again on my shoulder. In a move that may have been taught, the way they all did it. 'He was killed, beta, by some militants. We don't know whether by some other group, or ...'

There had been news of militants, separatists, whatever we were supposed to call them, being killed by rival groups.

'Or maybe, we have some such information; maybe he was killed by his own group, by the leaders, or by those who didn't like his leadership, if he was a leader. Beta, we need to know, we will find your father's killers if … if … you can give us some information.'

He repeated the question. Did I know that my father was a terrorist? A man who spread death, destruction, despair – atank?

'He left us sir; we don't know where he went. My ammi says, said, that he, he …'

How could I give tongue to the same lie about his being involved with another woman? 'He didn't tell us anything, sir, just left us, sir.'

'Hmm … !'

They obviously had the other details about when he had left, maybe, even about our attempts to get help from Aman.

'Son,' the officer said gently, 'son, I know you'd like to be alone just now. But time is something we may not have enough of …,' he stopped, waited for me to ask, so I did, 'what?'

'Just now, your mother was screaming about her son, she was saying, where is my son …'

'Yes?'

'What is this about? Where is your brother, is he not with you?'

The noose tightens. Do I tell him about Umed, about Hameed? By telling, will I be getting him into trouble, or worse? But images of my little boey spring to my mind. Alone, without the father he had set out to find, so wanted to be with. Given up everything he knew to go to. Now alone. With Abbu gone, dead, who would look after him now? Maybe, just maybe, if I were to tell this man, he could help us find Umed, bring him back to safety. To us. Should I tell – should I tell?

'Tell me about your brother, beta, tell me a bit about him.'

'Like what?'

He guided me to sit on the top step. Where Abbu and I had sat. Before. And he persuaded me to tell him all about Umed. How old he was. 'How young!'

What class he studied in.

That he was good at his studies. 'Ah what a waste.'

'And now, where is he now?'

'He, he also left, like Abbu.'

'And your mother let him?'

'What could she do, he was determined.'

'But he was just a child. I can understand she couldn't stop your father, but the child?'

I didn't say anything. What was there to say?

'And did he find him? Did you get news he reached your father's outfit?'

'No, we never heard anything once he'd left.'

'And you never worried? The child, the little child was all alone.'

Maybe there was something in my expression. Although I didn't say anything, or even shake my head, he caught on immediately.

'He was not alone?'

I looked at him surprised.

'Who was with him?'

Who indeed – who was with him? I knew no more than his name, and even that could have been false.

'Did your father come for him?'

I shook my head.

'Did he send someone for him?'

I shook my head again. It was not a lie. Abbu sent Hameed to deliver money, not to get Umed.

'Why did your younger brother go and not you?'

I shrugged my shoulders, 'why indeed?' It was a question I'd asked myself many times. I didn't have an answer, at least not a completely honest one.

'Beta you will have to answer my questions. You know, we need some answers from you. It's your choice. You can either give me your answer now, tell us the truth. Or I'll have to ask your mother, force her to re-live very difficult, painful moments.'

As if she needed anyone else's help to feel more pain now!

'And if even that fails, we'll have to take you away for interrogation. Both of you. And believe me, you don't want that.'

'But, but sir, I don't know how to answer your questions.'

'With the truth. That's all I want.'

'But I don't have the answers to the questions you ask.'

'All right, let me ask you some other questions then. Listen, think of each one carefully and give me those answers that you have – is that fair?'

It was fair. He warned me too, not to hold back information to tell me all I knew. And then the questions began.

'When your father left, did he tell you where he was going and why?'

'No, just said he had to go and was leaving me in charge of things.'

'You didn't ask?'

'Of course, of course, I did. But he didn't say.'

'Did he say why he had to leave?'

'It was something about a fight between him and Ammi. Actually, if I remember correctly, it was she who told him to leave.'

93

'But you're not sure why?'

'I–I had followed him without either of them knowing. I wanted to know where he was going, where he went every night. So I followed him but he caught me and brought me back. That's when Ammi said enough was enough. She said that he had to choose one or the other ...'

'One or the other, what?'

'I didn't know myself, then. But afterwards, Ammi told the army officer who came then, something about another woman. That's when I came to know the reason, the real reason for his going.'

'Rubbish! That's rubbish. He had become a terrorist, an atankvadi. Did you know that?'

I don't know if he expected any answer to that, so I shook my head in the negative. What was the point telling him that yes, we did know? What was the point of any of it now? The army man's questions brought me back to the present.

'After he left, son, has he been in touch with you at all?'

'No.'

'Tried to contact you with a letter, someone, a word, a phone call. Anything?'

'Nothing.'

'Did he send money to help you out? Things could not have been easy after he left.'

'Never, Ammi wouldn't have taken it even if he did, no matter how difficult we were finding it to manage.' I couldn't keep the bitterness out of my voice.

'Any idea where he had gone? Any inkling at all?'

'No.'

'Then son, how did your brother set off in search of him? Where would he even start to look for him if all that you say is true? He was a very young child. And Kashmir is a very big place. A dangerous place. Your father could be anywhere – he could be across the border. How did both of you – you and your mother – let him go off on this impossible, dangerous journey?'

I didn't know how to answer, so I hung my head down, knowing my story was full of holes.

'Look, son, obviously there was some contact made. I could have believed all you've said if your brother had not set off in search of him. He had to have some clue, some word as to where to go looking. You need to tell me. As I've said, you can do this the easy way or the hard way, but we will get the truth out of you. One way or the other.'

But I couldn't get a word out. Let Ammi decide how much or what was to be revealed. But when I glanced in, she was still bent over the prone cold body that was once her husband.

The army man saw me glance in. He knew I was hiding truths. He sighed, stretched out his legs, rubbed his hands together, then sighed again.

'Dekho beta, your little brother is alone now. He could be in grave, grave danger. These terrorist units are often short of man-power. They won't hesitate to use a boy, a child, your brother, to execute one of their diabolical plans. Now that he doesn't have his father's protection, he could be used.'

I looked at him, knew he was right. He continued.

'There have been cases, not too many, but not too few either, where very young children have been convinced they are doing God's work. Often, they're told there will be enough time for them to get away, once they've detonated an explosive device. They're told there will be other adults closeby to help them get away if something goes wrong. But there is no time – was never going to be. And there is no help at hand at all. Was never going to be.

'So if you want to save your brother, if you'd at least like to try, then your best chance is to tell us all you know. We are his best chance for safety ...'

'But suppose he gets hurt?'

'Yes, there is a chance he may get hurt. It could happen. But if we leave him there, then there is no doubt he will get hurt – probably killed. They will use him. If he tries to protest, or if he refuses, they'll have no use for him at all. They will kill him. I'm not guessing any of this; we've seen it all before, all too often. But, if you give us a lead, we will try to crack this militant outfit, we will try to find them. Maybe find your father's killers too. And for my part I can promise you that I will keep a lookout for him and will personally take every precaution to see that he is not harmed. I cannot promise anything, but I will do my best to bring him back to you, to your mother.'

The truth comes out

And so the truth came out. What else could I do but tell him everything? Although everything wasn't much at all. About Hameed and his bag of money. And about Ammi's ultimatum when Umed wanted to go with Hameed to Abbu.

'But I think she'd let him come now …,' I ended, not telling him Hameed had been persuaded by Ammi to give up the path of terror and return to his own home. What would have been the use of revealing that? He, at least, was probably safely home now.

Abbu was buried later that day. With me performing his last rites. Both Ammi and I were dry-eyed, for we'd shed all the tears we had for him already. He had been dead for us long ago.

Ammi understood I had told them all about Abbu's leaving, then Hameed's arrival and departure with Umed. I could tell that he, the army man was impressed by the fact that she returned the money. I think it helped in clearing us of any impending suspicion he had. It convinced them we would have no links with the outfits, whatever and whoever they were.

Bas, all that was left now, was to look for Umed. Ammi gave some photographs of him. She even blessed the army people and wished them godspeed and good luck in their mission to get the terrorist who had lured Abbu away and bring Umed back to safety.

And then, the little glimmer of hope for Umed was the only thing that changed as we went back to the dreariness of our existence. That and Ammi's stranglehold on my every movement, every moment, which became ever-increasingly tighter, if that was possible.

One day, when we got home after she had picked me up from work, we found a letter awaiting us. Ammi opened and tried to read it, but found that her eyes were blurring and she couldn't make the words out. So I read the letter out to her.

Hameed was home! It was a letter of thanks. From Hameed to Ammi for showing him the right path. Thanks also came from Hameed's mother who confessed she had given up hope of ever finding her son alive again. She said, 'You are his mother too now. For you have given birth to my son, given him a new life all over again.'

Ammi smiled and laid her head on my shoulder and whispered she hoped Allah would reward her good deed by bringing her own son back as well. That evening, the house was fragrant with the aroma of halwa she made for both of us. Although could see the inquisitive woman next door looking through our window with disapproval, her hand raised to her mouth, we just smiled at each other as Ammi drew the curtain, cutting her disapproval out of our sight. We both knew the news would travel fast around the neighbourhood. That we were feasting although Abbu's death was not yet a month ago.

I thought, now she was in a better mood than she had been in a long time, I would broach the question that had been on my mind for a long time.

'Ammi,' I began as we washed the dishes that night, 'Ammi, I've been thinking ...'

'What has my beta been thinking?'

'Although I work very hard in this job of mine, they're not paying me much.'

She started to say something, but I wanted her to let me finish.

'See, I know they're not going to pay me much more, no matter how long or how well I work. It's just such, such unskilled work. I sweep and dust and fold all day long.'

'Its good work and you should be happy to have it.'

'Yes, yes, I am happy. But Ammi, I'm better than that, no? See, I can read and write. I even know English a bit, I was good at it in school, so ...'

'So what are you saying, now you're too good to work for Ghulam Rasool bhai who was kind enough to give you employment when we were desperate?'

'Just listen to me, please, Ammi.'

'Hmm ...'

'Ammi, I'd, I'd like to try to find a better job.'

'No.'

'No?'

'No.'

'Just like that – no? You haven't even heard me, you haven't even listened.'

'I feel safe with you here. I know Ghulam Rasool will not let any harm come to you. He won't let any bad men get to you.'

'Oh Ammi, he doesn't let *anyone* get to me. I don't get to meet anyone who comes to the shop. I barely even see anyone's face, except Ghulam Rasool's and yours.'

'Good.'

'Good? Do you know how stifling it is? Not to go anywhere, talk to anyone, see anyone, even. Sometimes, sometimes, at night, when I'm on my own, I say my name out loud because I'm desperate to know I'm a person – I need confirmation I exist at all.'

'Ghulam Rasool doesn't pay to entertain you, he pays you to ...'

'But he barely pays me anything. What's the use of my having given up school to just earn such a paltry sum, when I could earn more?'

We argued back and forth. Although I could see how adamant she was and knew she didn't often budge once she got like that. I wasn't willing to give in so easily either. She had to see how difficult this was for me.

So I told her my education and hard work all those years in school should be put to better use. Tourism was picking up finally in the valley. I had overheard a customer who'd come to the shop, a man who worked as a waiter in a hotel, say that they were fully booked for the whole season. That tourists were blessing the Kashmir valley once again, hopefully ending to the drought of the past almost ten years. He had said there were people from all over India as well as foreigners pouring in. There a was huge demand for tourist-related services.

I could paddle a shikara boat – take tourists through the Dal and Nagin lakes. That's what I wanted to do more than anything. Be on the water, talking to people, hearing about their lives, the world out there. Feeling the fresh breeze bathing my face, the expanse of the big blue sky above. And even more than that, feeling my muscles work and build with every pull of the paddle.

'Please Ammi.'

'No.'

She went through her whole litany of the 'dangers out there' yet again. And then burdened me with further guilt by saying, 'At least wait till Umed comes back. Then I'll think about it.'

And that was that.

A last ray

I was cleaning the counter top at the shop, awaiting Ammi's arrival. I glanced at the newspaper, but before I could read anything, Ghulam Rasool clicked his tongue and looked pointedly at the clock. Ammi was late again. She'd been getting late often these days. The house where she worked had a wedding coming up. Relatives were already arriving and work had increased. But obviously my employer needed to get to his home, but he'd promised to wait until she came to fetch me.

'Janaab, don't worry, I can wait here on my own.'

'No, no, I can't leave the key with you.'

'You can lock up, sir. I'll wait for her right outside the shop, sir.'

'But I promised, I promised to stay with you till she comes.'

'And you've always kept your promise, sir. And Ammi is very grateful for it, as am I, but … ' Suddenly the prospect of being able to be on my own, just on my own, unwatched outside the four walls of my house seemed, like a huge treat. I wanted him gone as quickly as possible. Don't get me wrong, I wasn't going to do anything other than wait, just wanted to wait alone for a few precious minutes.

'But …,' he said, looking at the clock again.

'Janaab, I won't step out on the street at all. I will sit on the top step, sir.'

He said he'd rather wait, but ten minutes later, when there was not one thing left to do in the shop and no sign of Ammi, he stood and told me he really had to leave. He made me promise not to go beyond the steps leading to his shop, not to so much as make eye contact with a soul. To keep my head down until Ammi came.

'Sir, then can I take the newspaper – I'd like to practise my reading, it's been so long since I left school, I may just forget all I've learnt.'

He agreed, saying it would keep me from looking up and engaging with strangers. He left me with many a dire warning, and even as he strode away, he kept looking back until he finally turned the corner. I know because I watched from the corner of my eye. When he was finally gone, I lifted my head. I felt light, as though a great weight had been lifted off me.

I was alone. Alone at last. No anxious eyes keeping me prisoner. I looked around as though looking at the world through new eyes. I even, inadvertently, smiled at a passerby before remembering the many promises I'd made to my employer and mother. So I unfolded the newspaper and read about what was happening in the world beyond my own little life.

And that's when I saw his picture – Hameed's – on the front page.

'Innocent bystander killed by terrorist group. Links suspected' ran the headline, but then, just then, Ammi came, rushing up to me. 'Sorry, sorry. I saw that army man who'd come to our house. I went to him to ask about Umed — whether they had any word.'

'And?'

'No, nothing. But, but what are you doing out here alone? Why aren't you inside, why isn't . . .'

'Ammi, Ammi, Ammi, it's all right, shh! Calm down, Ammi. He had to leave.'

'But why should he be so careless? I told him, requested him, he promised me . . .'

I guess I could have taken the opportunity to say yes, he was careless and she should now let me explore other avenues of employment, but she was already so fraught that I just folded the paper under my arm, put my other arm around her shoulder and led her home. Reassuring her that Ghulam Rasool had just left. I'd hardly been alone at all. I'd not done anything to attract attention, nor been given any.

When we got home, I made some salted tea to revive her and put the rice on to boil, knowing she would soon come out with the story of her meeting with the army man. It had left her a little more broken, I could see. The more time elapsed with no news of Umed, the bleaker the chances became of finding him. Of finding him safe.

I secreted the newspaper away. Although I was dying to read it, know more about what had happened, I knew this would wound her hope even more.

'Yah Allah,' she continued, 'I can see only one ray of hope, Umer.'

'What's that Ammi?'

'Hameed.'

'But he's gone,' I blurted out before I could stop myself. But she took my gone as gone home, no ... not ...

'Yes, but he'll know their movements, their hideouts. I think the time has come for us to go to him, take his help. He'll be able to lead us to Umed. At least, at least, he's our best chance.' She finished bleakly.

'How will we ever find him, Ammi? The letter didn't have an address and in any case, it must have been thrown away by now.'

'No, no, I kept it.'

'But do we know where he lives?'

'He mentioned Kupwara when we talked and there'll be a postmark on the outside.'

'Ammi – Kupwara's a big place. And what will we do with a postmark? Really Ammi.'

'It's not much, but it's still our best chance, don't you see, Umed? I've been thinking, suppose you and me shut down the house, spring is not too far away now. We'll go in search of Hameed and when we find him, he'll help us, I know he will.'

Ah, now here was a challenge indeed, I didn't want to tell her about Hameed's death as yet, and she had to be told that her 'one last ray of hope' was dead.

How could I tell her? How was I going to tell her? I would have to, of course. 'But Ammi ...'

'Why can't you just support me on this? Why are you insisting on being difficult?'

'Because it's not going to lead anywhere, you have to stop believing foolish things.'

'Then what would you have me do – should I just forget I had another son? Forget that he could be in huge, huge danger? You'd have me do that, would you? You may have given up your brother for dead – but I'll never, never give up on my son. Never.'

Her sudden anger was melting into tears – despair. Spiralling into the abyss that was dark and deep. She was looking at me accusingly, as though it was my fault Umed wasn't with us today. A thousand counter accusations tingled on the tip of my tongue. I wanted to shout out, 'it was you who let him go. It was you who made him choose between Abbu and you. It was you who said he couldn't come back. Now you want him back. But it's too late, too late, too late.'

My anger matched hers, measure for measure, but I didn't say anything. I knew she wasn't blaming me; really, her anger was directed at herself, the blame squarely on her shoulders. She knew it; she didn't need me to remind her. But she did need somewhere to put the heavy burden of guilt, if only for a little while. I knew all this, but I was still angry. Over so many things. And I still savoured the lingering fleeting moments of freedom I had experienced just a little while ago. I wanted more of it, needed it.

I needed to get away from her before I blurted out all that I had in my heart. I picked up the newspaper from under the carpet where I had slipped it when I was taking off my shoes. I wanted to know what had happened. I hoped for Ammi's sake that the news was wrong or that I'd mistaken the boy in the picture for Hameed. That it was someone else who'd been killed. It had only been a fleeting glimpse, after all.

But there was no mistake, Hameed had been killed. The picture of the body was distorted but there was an inset of a picture from an ID card. There was no mistake. It was Hameed all right. The article said the boy, the 'victim' probably had links with the terrorists who had killed him although his family claimed his innocence. Reading through the whole thing, a second time over, I put the pieces of the puzzle together as best I could. And a picture emerged.

Hameed had probably been followed, and found by members of the group he'd tried to leave at Ammi's insistence. He had been able to get away, to reach home, but then they had found him. And they were right after all, all those people who said there was no getting away once you were in it. He was actually safer with the group than at home. Oh, this was going to be yet another burden on Ammi's shoulders.

I looked at the photograph again. How dead he looked. His blood was a dark patch next to him. His mouth was open. His eyes were open too. He had been taken completely by surprise.

Now how was I going to tell Ammi? Her hopes, her fast-fleeing hopes were pinned on Hameed giving us some clues, some direction to follow. How was I going to tell her?

A whiff of freedom

It was done. She was told. She had her breakdown. She had her tears, her fears. Again. This roller coaster was relentless, with more downs and hardly any ups at all. It seemed we were going steadily down, down, down. And every time we reached an abyss and thought that we could sink no more, we'd be sucked into a depth even further. The blows wouldn't stop raining on us.

And with each one, with each loss, Ammi's grip on me tightened. Fearing she was going to lose me too, she held on to me so tight I was completely choked. It was like she was drowning and I was the one thing she could hold on to keep afloat. I could understand that, of course, but it didn't make it any easier on me. It was killing me to be kept on such a short leash. Days and days would go by without my talking to anyone. Anyone, literally. Ghulam Rasool had no time for chatter with his lowly assistant. It was just salaam waleh kum in the morning and khuda hafiz or shaba khair at night.

Once a month I said 'shukriya' when he handed Ammi my pay. Yes, the money was given to her. Never to me. Even though the pay was such a pittance, it wasn't as if I could do anything too exciting with it. But I was not to be trusted with anything, although I was the one in Ammi's life, the only one, really, who had proved to be trustworthy, the only one who hadn't broken her trust. So, in fact, I bore the brunt of everyone else's every broken promise, every false hope and every shattered dream.

But I was finding it too hard to be with her any more. It was getting too hard to play the part of the good son. I didn't feel good, I didn't want to be good. I had dreams of my own. And deep in secret sleep, I knew the time was approaching for me to go after them.

'It's my cousin's birthday,' I lied to Ghulam Rasool one morning. 'I need to make a call to him to wish him ....'

He hesitated, I added for emphasis, 'Ammi says I must, she says we must keep up with our relatives, there's no one else.' I knew he was a tight fisted man, so I continued, 'They live in Delhi now, they left some time ago, years .... I need to call Delhi.' No way was he going to let me make a call to Delhi from his own phone.

'I can't let you make a call to Delhi from here, these calls are very expensive, you know.' I knew they were not very expensive, but I had rightly banked on his tight-fistedness to let me go. There was no cousin in Delhi to call, no birthday, no celebration. I just needed to get out of the shop, just for a little while. After that tiny taste of freedom, I needed more. Like a drug I needed to taste once again.

He hesitated, again remembering the promises made to Ammi. Besides, he would not want me to have even a little free time during my working hours, if he could help it.

'I'll go during my lunch break. You don't even have to give me lunch, I've already eaten too much at breakfast. You know the house that Ammi works in has a wedding, they sent lots of leftover food for us. I ate that, I'm not at all hungry now.' Amazing how easily the lies were spinning off my tongue. I'd never been much of a liar, never needed to be. Now, all of a sudden, I was an expert at it. 'I'll be quick, just wish him and bas, I'll be right back and at work. Don't even need a full lunch break, since I'm not eating.' Of course I'd be hungry, but it was a small price to pay. And I was more than willing to pay it. There were other hungers that needed satiating too.

Success, the sweet taste of it, the sweet taste of freedom. I walked out and a breeze started up immediately, it was as if it blew specially for me, to celebrate my precious new freedom, the few moments of it. I turned back, and, sure enough, I saw Ghulam Rasool staring out of the door, suspiciously at me, I nodded in acknowledgement, then went straight to the phone booth, I knew I'd better pretend to make a phone call, for he was quite capable of checking I did. I waited, looking at new faces, listening to a woman making a call to some distant loved one. It was as if a whole world was slowly blossoming before me, for me. A real world, beyond the jail life I was living. The woman on the phone burst into peals of laughter. Taken by surprise, I also started to laugh; it had been such a long time since I'd heard that kind of laughter. I couldn't help it, as she dissolved into giggles, I did too. She gave me a funny look and turned away, suddenly sobering up. But my giggles continued.

The man in charge of the booth smiled, 'What's the matter brother, what is it that you find so funny?' he said it kindly, nothing more, just passing time, really. I just laughed some more and said it was good to laugh. They all thought I must be some kind of a maniac. But I didn't care. I got up, still giggling and began to leave the shop. 'Where are you going, brother, did you not have a phone call to make?'

'Er ... yes, I – I forgot to bring the number, don't worry, I'll get it and be back later. Khuda hafiz.' He gave me a strange look. But I did not want to spend my precious moments cooped up in yet another shop.

So I stepped out into the sunshine once more. The warmth of it on my back, the breeze on my face were like long lost friends embracing me, caressing me. Suddenly I didn't really care if my employer guessed I had lied, that there was no phone call made. I wasn't doing anything bad, just walking, just looking, breathing, being. I passed a vendor selling roasted chestnuts, their nutty aroma fragrancing the air. I didn't have any money on me, not a paisa, but there was nothing to stop me from filling my stomach with the warm perfume of it. I smiled at the man, and he smiled back. 'Buy some chestnuts, beta, they're the best you'll find.'

'Yes, they look very fine, but I don't want any right now.' We got into a conversation, he told me where he got the chestnuts from and I told him I worked in the shop around the corner. It was a nothing conversation, but it meant the world to me. Eventually, the man picked up a twist of paper and shovelled some of the warm nuts into the funnel. 'Here, take some, they're good.' Of course I protested, I refused, said that I was not hanging about wanting charity, but he insisted and swore it would give him happiness to see a young boy eat.

'My own son has gone away, so ...,' he said wistfully as I cracked open the first nut.

'Where?'

'I sent him away, beta. There's nothing here for young boys to do nowadays. No jobs worth anything, just trouble looking to find a young boy like him.'

'Why, you can't say that, the tourist season is booming, every hotel, every houseboat is booked, so they say.'

'Ah, but there's the safety factor also, no? Every time he was away, I'd be worried sick if he'd come back.'

'You sound just like my mother,' I laughed.

'Yes, and she's right you know. What about your father, then, doesn't he worry?'

'He ... he ...'

'Oh, I'm sorry, I understand. It's these damned terrorists spreading their atank, they don't leave anyone untouched, not even apne kaum ke log one's own community. Here, here, take some more chestnuts.'

Now it really was charity. Pity food, I didn't want it. Suddenly the warmth of the chestnuts, the warmth of their aroma, turned cold, the taste bitter. Enough, I didn't want any more. But he was pressing another twist of nuts into my hands. This one more loaded than the last. But I didn't want it, couldn't take it. What would I tell Ghulam Rasool, why was I loitering about in the market, when I'd just had to make a phone call. And what would I tell Ammi?

I ran, the vendor calling after me, 'Here take them son, don't be like that ...'

I ran, my freedom burning to ashes.

I ran, the flight of freedom leaving a noose to tighten around my neck and I was stifling. I burst into the shop, panting, panicking.

'What? What happened? What happened?'

'Nothing, nothing. I – I – just ...,' the lies weren't flowing so easily now.

'Oh, I knew I shouldn't have let you out. But what happened, something happened, what is it?'

'No, no, it's just that ... it's just that I thought I'd taken too long, that you'd be worried. There was a queue; it took very long for the phone.' My heart was calming down now and the lies could spin once more.

'And did you make your call? Did you wish your cousin?'

'No, no, I couldn't get through ... the number was engaged, that's why it took so long. I'm sorry.'

'Doesn't matter son, here, why don't you eat something, I kept a little rice and aul for you from my lunch. You will be hungry.'

'No, sir, I'm not hungry at all.' I couldn't face food right now.

'Come on, a growing boy like you. Of course you're hungry. And something panicked you, didn't it?' He fussed about, being more caring and concerned than he'd ever been. 'I'm going to speak to your mother and tell her she shouldn't send you off on errands like making phone calls. Sometimes women don't realize exactly how dangerous it can be for young boys. Even in broad daylight.'

I was appalled. I hadn't thought of this.

I begged him not to. Used all my newly acquired skills of lying, telling him I did not want to worry her. She had enough of that as it was. I needed to help her sometimes, rarely though, with some little chores. She was so exhausted she could collapse any time. I assured him I was careful and that he should not worry and that he should definitely not bother Ammi with his unfounded concerns.

He swallowed it. Of course, a good part of it was true, but still. Amazingly, as I folded up the goods strewn around by a customer, I didn't feel in the least bit guilty. Why should I, I reasoned. I had done nothing wrong. Nothing wrong at all. They were all just being too cautious. Nothing was going to happen. Nothing ever did, to me, personally. I was boringly safe.

Nevertheless, when Ammi came to collect me later, I hung close to her, urging her I wanted to get home, that I needed to use the toilet urgently. Yet more lies skimming seamlessly off my lying tongue. My employer though, was in an affable mood. He praised me and said I was an honest, hard-working boy and that Ammi should be very proud to have a son like me. No, not a pang of guilt troubled me even then.

'Ammi, chalo, I really need to go to the toilet, let's go, please,' I whispered.

'Aachaa Ghulam Rasool, bhai, once again, thank you for all your kindness,' she said finally, making to leave.

'And yes, behenji, my best wishes to your nephew on his birthday as well.'

'My nephew … ?'

'Ammi … !!!'

The truth came out. Of course it would. It was awful, but Ammi covered up for me the best she could. She pretended to go along with the lie, that there actually was a cousin to call. If Ghulam Rasool had his suspicions, he kept them to himself. Ammi smiled and lied till we were in the shop. She was silent as we walked, one behind the other. Me in front, she keeping an eye on my every move from behind.

But when we got home, she beat me.

Breaking away

I'm not going to take it any more. The questions. The suspicions. The shoutings. The looks. The sulking. The muttering hateful things under her breath. The lies. That's what I hate the most. The web of lies is so thick I don't remember what I told her the day before yesterday, or the day before that. The web of lies so thick I can't see my own way out of it any more. So I get tongue-tied today.

'Shifty-eyed,' she calls me, 'you've become shifty-eyed. You can't meet my gaze any more, can't look me in the eye. You've got too much to hide.' Then, as though it's the very worst insult, she says, 'You've become just like your father!'

Said with so much hate and disgust. As though telling me that I've become a rat, or worse, a filthy pig.

Her hold on me tightens, tighter than ever before. Plus she is angry and suspicious all the time. *All the time.* At first I tried to explain to her why I'd done it. That I felt the need to get away sometimes. Tried to remind her that I was the one, the only one, who had not let her down. That I had stood by her in the past and was continuing to do so. So she needed to have a little faith in me too. Tried to tell her I was too young to lead this life of non-existence. But she never heard me, never wanted to. Maybe she couldn't, who knows?

She was beyond reason. And I was beyond caring. For her. For my own safety, for anything, except my own need and desperation to be free.

And I know now – for sure – that it is time to leave. Someone will look after her. She'll manage. I would help her manage, but she's having none of it. 'Don't ever bring blood money into my house,' she says. Over and over again. Like a prayer. 'If I'd been weak, if I'd had no principles, we may have been rich, we'd have been rich by now, living in one of those fancy houses that people are building all over Kashmir. Big houses, so big that there's no one to fill them. If I had been willing to compromise, your father may even have been alive … but we'd be living a wrong life, an evil life.'

There's no point telling her that we were better off then. No point saying that's the way we would have preferred it, Umed and I. And she should have listened to us. She should have listened to us, trusted us. Her own husband, her own sons. She had lost two of them and now she was about to lose the last of us. What good were these principles of hers? How did it matter what was done to earn it, where the money came from? Money was money. It didn't have black or white stamped on it, good or evil. It was, after all, money. And it bought you things you needed, wanted, desired, lusted for. It bought you comfort and peace of mind.

But now, there's nothing. None of the above. We are the Unwanted. Weeds.

So one day, I decided to break free. I had to, you have to understand. I left safety, strangling safety. I planned for it carefully. I took a little money, secreting it away from Ammi, from the shop, telling myself it was mine anyway. Or at least that it was her fault. It wasn't much, but it was a start. I also kept aside some bits of food. Raw rice, kulcha, bakarkhani, nuts, whatever could last a bit. Whatever would not be missed too much. I hid bundles in the shop so that there would not be too much to carry at one time, once the time for the break actually came.

Saying goodbye was suddenly surprisingly hard. Surprising because I had been so angry with her I forgot I loved her so much as well. Looking at her now, as she bustled about, getting us ready for the day, folding bedclothes, hanging up the clothes she'd already washed although it was still early in the morning, chopping, frying food, packing a little lunch for me. It was endless. I thought I helped out a lot around the house and now, I suddenly realized how much she'd been doing. Invisibly. Or maybe, I didn't have the eyes to see it.

I want to console her, tell her she'll be all right. But of course, I can't. I hang on to her every movement. I hang on to the song she's humming under her breath. I haven't heard her do that for the longest time. Humming. Like a bird. Has she been singing all along and I didn't hear? I'm wracked with guilt, with a sense of responsibility. But I steel myself and steal away the food and money I've been secreting away. I try to re-kindle the hate I've been feeling for her. It sparks, it sputters, stutters and almost goes out. She turns as if I have spoken. She looks at me. I can't meet her gaze, not with these shifty eyes of mine. And then she is next to me, in front of me, feeling my forehead.

'What, what is it, beta? Are'nt you well, are you sick? What's happened suddenly?'

'N-n-nothing, nothing, oof ho, what are you doing?' I bat her work-roughened hand away.

'Don't try to fool me, beta, there's something wrong. I'm your mother, I know.'

'Come on, let's go, we'll be late for work.'

'Tell me, oh tell me, beta, what is it? Something's wrong. I know it. Please tell me, I'm your mother, you can tell me anything.'

'There's nothing wrong, why should you think there is?' This was unnerving, how had she sensed something was wrong?

'Beta, your face is so tense, so pale ...'

'You don't allow me out into the sun; between you and Ghulam Rasool, you've made me into a creature of the darkness, that's why I'm pale, obviously no?'

She didn't say anything; she put her hand to her mouth. Her eyes widened, as though in shock, or recognition. It was as if, in that moment, she understood everything, what my intentions were. That she was going to be on her own now.

'What?' I snapped, turning away, trying to get away from her prying gaze.

'You're right, you're right my son. Oh my poor, poor son. What have I done to you?'

'Ammi, look, we'll talk about this later, we must be getting on to work now.'

She stared at me, as though looking at me for the first time. Noticing me for the first time. I wished she wouldn't. All this time when I had longed for her notice, acknowledgement, she hadn't given it to me. Why now, I wondered, why now?

But she continued to look at me, look straight into my eyes, my soul, seeing the secret I was desperately trying to hide.

Remembering what happiness is

'No,' she said, 'let's not, let's not ...' She smiled her little girl smile, the one I hadn't seen for a long, long time.

'What? Let's not what? I don't know what you're talking about my Ammi jaan, and we don't have time to linger and chat. We must get to work, you and I. Let's go now.'

'No,' she repeated, her smile like a naughty child's, 'let's not go to work, you and I. Let's phone and tell them we are unable to come to work today. I'll say I'm sick and you say you're sick.'

'What? My dear honest mother is becoming a liar?'

'Yes, yes, for once, let's just lie, anybody can fall ill and you and I have taken no leave, not a minute's leave, ever. So let's do it now.'

'And do what? What would be the point?'

'We could spend the day in the sun. We could take a bus to Nishat Bagh, we could eat some delicious food along the way. I know, we could go to the Hazrat Bal mosque and eat in the little shops there. We'll say our jummah namaz there as well. Oh what a great idea, what fun we're going to have.'

She was already stripping off her dull heavy grey working phiran, she rushed to the box where she kept her clothes and was rummaging about in it pulling out the brighter ones she hadn't worn since Abbu left, perhaps even longer.

'Come on, come on,' she urged, 'get some nice clothes out. We're going to get you some sun, we're going to put some colour back into your cheeks. Come on,' she almost shouted in her excitement, as she turned around and saw me rooted, dumbstruck. 'Let's not waste even a minute.'

Well, what was I to do? My plans of running away and making my own future lay in pieces on the ground. What was I to do? So I got my best clothes on and hid away the things that were to see me through the first few days of my new life. I felt excited and resentful at the same time. Excited because I had not been on such an outing with Ammi ever, I mean, never just the two of us. It had been all four of us. Then. Now we were just the two of us, playing happy family. I know I shouldn't be so bitter now, not when Ammi was taking me out for a day of sunshine and laughter. But I was resentful too. I felt as though she had stolen my life away from me, yet again. First, when she had shut me up in her own insecurity and now, again, when I had decided to live my life on my own terms, she'd reclaimed me back. It wasn't fair at all. But, what was I to do?

We made our phone calls. Neither of our employers were happy. I think Ammi got an earful although she was careful not to let on that she had, but some of the joy left her face. 'Look, if you have to go, if they're going to make things difficult for you, then, then, just go to work. We can always have our outing another time.' It was a weak attempt and I knew, in heart of hearts, that she was not going to change her mind.

'They can go to hell!' she said determinedly, and then the naughty child smile came back to her lips and eyes. She was not given to cursing, strongly objected when Abbu sometimes did and smacked us if either of us brothers cursed. But here she was, sending her employers to hell and feeling quite gleeful about it! I couldn't help feeling happy myself, in spite of myself. 'Okay,' I said, taking her by the hand, 'let's go then.'

We caught the bus to Nishat Bagh. It was like seeing the world for the first time – it was like being born again, into a new, beautiful world. There was not a trace of unhappiness and regret in my mother. She was shining as though happiness radiated from her. She could hardly contain her happiness, 'Look, look,' she chortled, 'look, there's the garden your Abbu and I used to walk in when we were first married. And, oh, that's where I fell when I was pregnant with you. It was so funny, because I was so heavy and your Abbu couldn't lift me up himself.'

'Didn't anyone come to help?'

'Of course, of course they did. But your Abbu didn't want any other man touching me, so …'

'So then, what did you do?'

'I kept laughing and sitting there, every time I'd try to get up, I'd start laughing all over again, and fall back down.' Tears of remembered laughter were coursing down her cheeks. She wiped her eyes with the corner of her head scarf as she continued, 'Eventually, it was another pregnant lady who picked me up with Abbu's help. By this time, the whole park was laughing. I was laughing, but I was also so embarrassed. After that, I refused to come to this park for a walk, although my doctor kept telling me walking was good and would make the delivery easy.'

'And was it?'

'What? The delivery? You? No, no, you were so reluctant to come out into the world, you just wouldn't leave your Ammi's insides!'

'Just like I am now,' I thought, 'still reluctant to go out into the world, still reluctant to leave my mother.' And when I was ready, there was this sudden turn of events and instead of seeking my own future, I was going on a picnic with my ammi.

But she didn't notice my thoughts, the downturning of my mouth, she jumped up, almost shouting, 'Roko, roko, this is our stop. Stop, stop, this is where I want to get off.'

'Shh, Ammi, what are you doing?'

The bus careened to a halt and she got off still laughing. 'Ammi, behave yourself, what are you doing? People are staring at you.'

'Let them stare, it's good for them.'

'Good for them?'

'Yes, they're not used to seeing such happiness and laughter anymore, hain na? So let them stare and remember what happiness is!' And with that, she gaily set off towards a park that bordered this corner of the Dal Lake. She knew this area well. This is where she had grown up. Nishat Bagh. We walked in the park looking at the people there, tourists, romancing couples and the fishermen coming in with their early morning catch of fish from the lake, carp, mostly. Then the muezzins from the Hazrat Bal mosque gave a call and it was time for the Friday namaaz.

When we came out, the air was fragrant with the aromas of frying pakodas and halwa, voices competed with each other, each trying to outsell the other. Ammi and I met up and then joined the throng. We moved towards the food stalls. What we didn't notice, in all the excitement, was a figure who kept his eye on us and made a move towards us as we moved further away from the mosque and into the crowd. In the meantime, the security men kept hawks' eyes on the crowd, on the lookout for just such a man.

'Ammi, wait here, I'll get us some halwa,' I said to her. 'All right, you do that, and I'll get some chestnuts.' She handed me some money and we parted. As I pushed through the post-prayer crowd, a voice whispered into my ear, 'Umer ...' I was startled; I was no longer used to hearing my name. And now here, a voice, an unknown voice? No, the voice was familiar. Where had I heard it? In the shop? 'Umer,' the voice held a warning, 'don't turn around just listen carefully. If you understand, nod your head.' I froze, but the crowd pushed in on me. Despite the warning, I started to turn my head.

'Don't,' the voice hissed again. 'Don't try to look at me, not yet. If you understand, if you want to hear what I have to say, just nod your head and keep moving forward slowly.'

I nodded. Yes, this was the voice of a customer who came a couple of times to the shop

'We have been watching you, but it's been difficult to make contact.'

'Who ...?'

'We are your father's friends, colleagues, brothers.'

'But Ammi ...'

'Yes, yes, your Ammi will not let you talk to us. It is because of her that we have not been able to talk to you, to help you.'

'Then?'

'We can create a disturbance, it's no problem. We can distract her and you can bolt from here. We can give you work, more money than you can imagine, it's what your father wanted.'

I turned then, I couldn't help it, but the man moved behind me so swiftly, 'Don't look back.'

'Where's Umed? Where's my brother.'

'We can take you to him.'

'Is he safe?'

'He is where he should be.' The voice was reassuring, and although I heard a little warning bell inside my head, I felt reassured. Maybe I wanted to be.

'He is all right?'

'He is all right.'

'Okay, I want to see him, I want to know more.'

'You will need to meet up with us. Here and now, are you ready for that?'

'I'm ready, really, just tell me how?'

'Here's an envelope, there are some instructions and some money to help you get away. There will be an explosion a few moments from now. It will create a disturbance. Get away from your mother and then follow the instructions.' He pressed an envelope into my hand. I slipped the packet into my pocket, trembling with excitement, and fear.

'Are you sure you're willing to join us?'

I didn't need to think of the answer, to weigh the consequences. 'Yes, yes, a thousand times, yes.'

'Good, fine …'

Someone is starting to push; the people at the back are getting impatient for their halwa.

But I needed to know, I couldn't help myself, 'How did Abbu

die?' But there was no answer. I turned; there were teeming crowds all around, how was I to know which one was the right man? I peered into some of the faces around me. I tried to detect some recognition in someone's eye, some acknowledgement, but there was nothing. Instead, one man shoved into me, saying, 'Hurry up will you, do you want the halwa or not?' I bought it, not with the money I'd just been given, but from what Ammi had given me. I was so excited, I wanted to get away. The time had come.

'See!' said Ammi as I went back to her, 'see, I knew a little bit of sun would be good for you, it's put the colour right back into your cheeks.'

Yes, my face was flushed, but it was not because of the sun. Now I really just wanted to get away, I wanted it to start. I slip my hand into my pocket and feel the envelope. It is my ticket to freedom. To a new life.

But then there was no more time to think.

'Fine,' the man said once I agreed to go with him. 'Fine. Now, here are the instructions,' he started to repeat his instructions once again, probably to ensure that I'd understood, 'there will be an explosion in a few moments. Separate yourself from your mother, she must not know any of this. Run towards the...' but he never told me, or I couldn't understand. For the man behind me was pushing. And then he was gone, without telling me where I was to run, or how Abbu had died. I needed to know that it was not them who had killed him. It couldn't be, wouldn't be. And yet.

Right then and there. There was an explosion, just as the man had promised there would be.

It was so loud I didn't know which way to turn, which way to run. So I just ran, blindly, without thinking. Hoping that they would somehow find me and tell me what to do. I ran, so this was running away day after all. I ran. And then I fell, headlong to the ground, something had hit me. A person? A splinter? I didn't know. I was running, then falling and then I passed out. It all happened so quickly and I could hear a voice in my head telling me to get up, that there was no time for lying on the ground. I had decided to make a getaway, and now, here I was just lying in a heap. I got up to move, but something dug into my side, sharp, like a knife. But I had to get up, had to find the man who'd spoken to me, who'd promised me that he'd take me to Umed. I had to get up. I didn't even know what he looked like.

'Don't move, don't move!' someone was shouting above, 'don't move!' But I had to. But I couldn't. The pain in my side was intense, the will and urgency to move forced me to try to get up, but instead, I passed out. The world receded and I knew that I had lost my best, brief half chance of getting away.

Wounds and worries

The next thing I knew, I could hear wailing, loud, long and pitiful. Someone must have died. I opened my eyes, but shut them quickly again, the light was too intense, my lids too heavy. The wailing and screaming continued. I tried to make out what the words were within the screaming. It was a name – *ah Mehmooda, Mehmooda, oh my Mehmooda*.

A man's voice, keening. Someone had died, Mehmooda had died. I tried to focus my thinking, did I know who Mehmooda was? But I couldn't remember. I could feel my mind sinking into the blissful state of unconsciousness again. But I couldn't faint again, I couldn't. I wanted to think, desperately. Water, I needed water, my mouth was paper-dry.

Then I could feel blessed water trickling through my parched lips, my tongue greedily licking up and absorbing the drops. I opened my eyes again. It was Ammi. I tried to speak and tell her about the man who had approached me. It was important that she knows and that we were close to finding Umed. But I couldn't speak. I saw Ammi join her hands in prayer, she murmured softly. She was praying and crying at the same time. Then she held my hand and lifted it to her eyes and broke down and wept, thanking God for my safe return, for my waking up. At last. At last? How long had it been?

As I regained strength and awareness, the truth came out, some snippets from Ammi, who, I could tell, wasn't telling me all of it. Some came from answers from the nurses when Ammi wasn't there and still more filtered through when the doctors and relatives of others were talking, although not directly to me. I filled in the jigsaw of information and made a rough picture of events.

So I knew there had been a huge explosion, many people were killed including some soldiers and jawans posted there to manage the rush of Friday prayers. Many were injured. I was one of them. The most frightening part of it was that the blast had taken place two weeks ago. Which meant I had been unconscious for fourteen days. I had lost fourteen days of my life. Worse, I had lost contact with the man who had apparently arranged the explosion, the one who was to take me to Umed. But, as I recalled the conversation he had with me, he had warned me to get away from my mother. His words, *your mother must know nothing of this,* sounded, so clearly I turned my head to see if he was there. But he wasn't. Then, I remembered the envelope of instruction and money he had pressed into my hands. I looked around for it. But it wasn't there. My stomach lurched with the thought that Ammi had found it, or someone else. But she never said anything and no one else came forward either.

As the pain abated, the plan slowly formed in my mind. The man had found me. I had not made any attempt to contact him, he had found me. Even on a day when we were on a completely unplanned trip to the mosque. When we should have been at work, Ammi and me. So that meant he or they, if there were more of them, were keeping an eye on us. They knew our movements. So, perhaps, they knew I was in hospital. They could contact me here as well and tell me what to do. Maybe they would take me now to Umed. But, I knew Ammi must not know. So I waited, looking closely at all those who came and went from this ward that had become my home. Especially when Ammi would go somewhere and leave me unattended, I hoped that they, he, would make a move and reveal himself to me. Give me further instruction.

But Ammi rarely left me. She was due to get some money as compensation for my injuries in the blast. Finally the tag of being family of a terrorist seemed to have receded and the government was going to give us some aid. So Ammi had taken leave from her work, maybe she would not get her job back as the house where she worked had found a replacement. I tried to exhort her to go on working, that I would be all right. But she was determined not to leave me more than necessary. She was practically camping outside the hospital, even boiling herself some rice as her meal on a makeshift chullah of mud and twigs. Sometimes Khalla brought her food or stayed with me while she went home to take care of things there, or just to bathe and rest. So I wasn't alone much, but they had still managed to get to me in the few moments I had been away at the mosque, so maybe they could manage it again. At any rate, I kept hoping they would.

In the meantime, the treatment continued and I was getting steadily better. I wasn't feeling better, though, for I knew I would soon be discharged and sent back home. Back to the prison that had become home. I knew it would be worse now after this. I knew and Ammi's mutterings confirmed my fears that, having almost lost me as well as the rest of the family, she was not going to let me out of her sight. She was barely going to let me draw a breath without her watching over me. It would become impossible for anyone to contact me then. As it is, they had been unable to get to me earlier.

Weed

My mind is made up. I will have to leave before the hospital discharges me. Because then Ammi will take me with her. I will leave whenever Ammi goes home. For once, luck is on my side and Khalla has gone to Delhi for her son's admission into college. So whenever Ammi goes, I am on my own.

'Ammi, go home, go get some rest, stay at home for the night and get a whole night's sleep instead of sleeping in the corridor outside.' I urge.

'Arre, Umer, do you think that I could sleep a whole night now? Do you think I'd be more at peace leaving you here? Do you believe there's any peace left, any home left within those four walls?' she insisted. 'I have no home now, except for you, with you.'

'Yes, but you look so pale and drawn, you must rest your body even if you cannot rest your heart.'

'My rest, my sukoon now lies in looking at you, looking after you, there is nothing more for me to do. I'm so sorry for the stupid suggestion I made that day. I don't care if you are pale and sunless, from now on, I will never let you out of my sight. I will not risk your life again for some foolish, dangerous outing.' She kept apologizing, agonizing over her decision of that day. This made me sure that I had to, had to leave. I knew now my life was going to be nothing more than a solitary one, in complete confinement. But she also kept thanking God for me, saying she would die if anything happened to me, her darling son.

She isn't making it any easier for me to do this. But I try to convince myself and tell myself that once I've brought her younger son home, she will have all the rest and sukoon she wants. I try to tell myself that I am only going away to search the mountains for Umed. I am only running away, giving her grief now, so she can get both her sons, her happiness, back later. Eventually, she is so exhausted that she agrees to go. I have thrown in the additional argument that my wages are pending with Ghulam Rasool, my old employer. She should go and claim the money that is rightfully ours. I tell her we will need the money for it will be a while before I can start working again. I reassure myself that with whatever is due from my wages and the compensation from my injuries, she will be all right financially until I get Umed and come back. Then we will see about continuing our lives and our sustenance. Until then, this is for the best, even if she doesn't know it and will fret and worry for now.

She goes, she wishes me goodnight. Again, yet again, I steel myself for the parting. It is hard and I hang on to her hand a fraction longer than normal, than I should. She has already started turning away, when she turns back and gives me a quizzical look. She smiles, she comes back to lean over me and kiss my forehead. 'You are so grown up, but you're still such a bachcha, a baby who wants his mother by his side. Do you want me to stay?'

I can see in her eyes that she half wants me to say yes, she wants me to want her. I do, oh Ammi, I do. But I shake my head and tell her to go, tell her to sleep peacefully so she can come back fresh tomorrow and look after me better. I have to close my eyes so she won't see the build up of goodbye tears. She laughs, tousles my hair and gives me a hug. I don't want to leave her, I think, know she needs me and oh God, I know that I need her. I wish I could hold her back, I wish it didn't have to be like this, I wish none of this had ever happened. I wish ...

And she is gone.

And so am I.

Stealing away into the darkness of the night, I have wrapped the one change of clothes I have with me and slipped my phiran on. The guard asks where I'm going and I tell him I want to pee in the open. It's been a long time, I joke. He laughs and yes, he agrees with me, peeing in these new fangled toilets is just not the same as watering the great outdoors. He is too sleepy to notice the bundle under my arm. He waves me off. My legs are stiff, my wounds have healed with the skin stretched taut and tight like clothes grown too small. It is freezing outside. I realize that I haven't been out in the cold darkness for a very long time. And suddenly I'm transported back to the awful night when it all began. The night I discovered the truth about my father and our home was torn asunder. I felt the same dread, the same feeling of not knowing what I was to discover, where I was to go and most of all, where this journey would lead and where would it end.

But I also knew that all the other options were closed to us. There was no support, no help forthcoming. And if no one out there was willing to help us, then we had to be our own helping hand, find our own way out of this morass. At least Abbu's people had come forward and offered to help. At least they had bothered to keep an eye open for us, despite Ammi's refusal to accept the help and money sent, they had still not given up on us, but had found a moment to come up and whisper in my ear and tell me they were willing to take me. When no one else was willing.

If there was no other way out, then I would follow in my father's footsteps, blighted though they may be, I would take the man's way, if I could no longer be a boy, a child. I would seek out my brother; I would seek out a better life for us where we could live with dignity and hope. I would be what my father had become, if that were the only way. I would be the weed, if that was the only thing I could become.

A weed, torn out from its own roots and cast aside. Only to find another little patch of land to dig in deep, grow new roots – a stronger weed than before.

Anew

He sneaks out into the darkness, the heart of a child beating like a child's, even though he convinces himself that he is a man. This time he has no money and no food. He does not know how he will sustain himself in the coming days. He does not know if they will come for him, find him. He does not know what to call his home, any more.

So he steals away into the darkness of his future, looking for a place to hide. The waters of the Dal Lake lap lazily. He can hear the waters rock a boat somewhere in the inky blackness. He sees a gate. There is enough of a gap for him to squeeze his childbody through the jointing. A lone light in one of the buildings warns him of human presence, but it is quiet, perhaps they are all asleep.

He runs alongside the houseboats that stand ready and warm for holiday-makers, those who come for the beauty of the valley.

He doesn't see the beauty any more. His eyes only search for darkness and invisibility.

Then he sees an old, broken houseboat. It is abandoned, it has to be. He creeps through the overgrown bracken and weeds, like a creature of the night. The boat sighs as though its age pulls it down. Or is it a sigh of welcome, of relief that it will have a visitor? More than half of it is sunk into the freezing black waters. But enough of it is above the water. Enough for him to make a hiding hole for himself. He pushes through the dense weeds that have not been breached since they grew here. He is at home amongst weeds. He steps cautiously on to the old houseboat. It creaks and rocks and seems to slip another inch towards its grave. He tests it to see if it will take his weight. Then, taking a firm grip on the rotting door jamb, he pulls himself into the boat. By the moonlight that filters in through the broken slats and missing windows, he sees signs of rotting grandeur. A carved roof and walls papered in an old English style. He treads the sloping floor, getting away from the rotting dampness of the parts thirstily absorbing water. He is exhausted. After his long stint in the hospital, he is no longer used to such exertion. His legs ache; his wounds cry out and beg him to stop.

He doesn't know what tomorrow will bring. How he will survive, sustain himself. How they will find him, if they are still looking. How will he find them, if they are not? Or, will someone else find him? He has heard of the encounters taking place. A man, even a boy lurking in dark suspicious places, would be a target in these torn and troubled times. But those are tomorrow's questions, today he must rest, he must make this boat his home.

He sinks to the floor and sighs. It is done, he must start his new life now. The boat sighs too. It is a friendly sigh, one that says, 'Welcome, you are home.' And he sleeps.

The yearning night

All through the yearning night, the mother's dreams are filled with running. She is chasing something, someone, but she does not know who she runs after. Or is it she who is running away and someone is chasing her? She runs in slush, in sleet, the thick ooze sucking her in, slowing her down. But she must not stop, she must not stop for it will be too late, she must keep running to catch up or escape.

All through the yearning night.

All through the yearning night, the boy's dreams are filled with running. He is trying to run back to his home. He is trying to run back into his past when he was a child and both his parents were there to look after his every need. Where his needs were no more than a new willow bat. All through the yearning night he yearns only for the years slipped away.

When she wakes up, it is with a start. With a deep sense of

loss as though a part of her has been amputated from her body. She looks down at herself, half expecting her body to have been mutilated. But she is whole, even though she feels incomplete, half. She wants to get back to Umer. Her Umer – long life, his name means. It is a name she and her husband chose with care. In these times of uncertainty, they blessed him with a name that signified years.

She must get back to him. But it is dark and the curfew will not release her from her house. She was foolish to have listened to her son. Of course there is no 'whole night's sleep', no sukoon and rest if she is so far from the only thing that keeps her drawing breath. Hurriedly she has a bath, barely feeling the freeze of the cold water on her back, not bothering to heat it before splashing it on to herself. Then she cooks some halwa with the little sooji she has left at home. She has no raisins and almonds for its garnish, she wishes she had, it would do him so much good. It will have to do. Then she ties it into a little bowl with a clean cloth. And then she sits by the door, waiting for the moment she can step out of the house. Willing the sun to rise quicker, earlier than it has ever before. It feels as though it is sleeping in late tonight. She won't take her eyes away from the window, waiting, waiting for the first sign of daybreak.

But before the day breaks, a new thought dawns on her. As she waits in the darkness, feeling imprisoned and impotent because she is unable to step out of her own free will, she is startled by the thought that this must be how Umer feels – imprisoned and frustrated – bound down by the darkness and twenty-four hour curfew she has imposed on him. A curfew without an end. Or hope of an end. This is why he made that excuse about the cousin's birthday and the phone call. He just wanted to do a small something out of his own free will. This is what he keeps trying to tell her. She smiles as she recalls the anger on his face when she refused to listen to the idea of his wanting to be a boatman. Yes, he is right. Although there are dangers, she has to let him lead his life. Let him live. After all, when the blast took place and he was hurt, why, he was right by her side! She had not been able to stop it from happening to him.

Yes, she decides, relieved to see the horizon glimmering with new light. She will have to loosen her hold on him. Before he makes some rash move and tries to run away. Yes, yes, he will be happy. She will tell him as soon as she gets to the hospital. How happy she's going to make him today.

When he wakes up, it is with a start. There is someone about – someone is close by. He can hear their voices. At first he doesn't know where he is. Completely disoriented, he is about to rush out and see who it is. But, just in time he remembers he is a runaway and looks around for a place to hide. But this sinking old houseboat has been stripped bare, there is nowhere to go, nowhere to hide. So he cowers as a face appears through a hole that was once a wall. It is an old, ancient face, so wrinkled that as if an old magician or wizard has come to life. The face wrinkles up even further as it frowns and smiles at the same time. The voice is as dry as autumn leaves, yet, strangely, as comforting.

'Ah, and who do we have here?' he laughs, stepping in and wheezing up the sloping floor as the boat slips a little further towards its watery grave. 'Oh dear, a little boy who seems to have run away. But you are not well, child, and you must be cold. And hungry.'

Umer just stares up at the stranger who seems to reveal his life as though he were reading about it in a book.

139

'How … ?'

'Come, come child, don't worry. Come with me, let's feed you first, get you warm. There'll be enough time for questions later. Come, come my son, don't be afraid. Come!'

There is a command in the old man's friendly voice Umer cannot ignore. He gets up stiffly and cannot stop the little cry that escapes as his legs cramp from cold, dehydration and their wounds. The man is back in an instant. 'Come, lean on my shoulders, just walk a bit, then you'll be fine.' He pulls Umer towards him, taking some of his weight on to himself. Although he is obviously very old, he is surprisingly strong. He is altogether surprising, the way he is so calm, so without suspicion at this stranger hiding, obviously wounded, obviously in trouble. Normally, in this abnormal world, the first instinct would have been to call in the police. Then, then Umer wonders, is he one of Abbu's men? He is about to ask, but just then the old man calls out, 'Aiyee, Farooque, we need some more chai and some hot food, son, look, we have a mehmaan today. It is a while since we have been blessed by a special guest,' he smiles at Umer, 'you know, we have had many foreigners, some Indians too, journalists and celebrities, but we have not had a Kashmiri guest for ever so long. You don't want to live in this houseboat son, it's falling to bits, no comforts left. You should pick one of the better ones, no?' He continues, pointing at the houseboats tied along the banks of the lake, polished and shining.

He makes Umer sit comfortably in the dark kitchen that smells of many years of feasts. The tea is given to him and the old man tells Farooque to heat up some potatoes and wangan from last night's dinner. He is behaving as though it is completely normal to find runaways in the area. Find them and look after them. Umer eats hungrily. It is only after a few mouthfuls that the tears come to his eyes. Again, the gentle old man seems to know what goes on in his head. He puts a wizened old hand on the boy's shoulder and strokes his back. 'Ah, the cooking reminds you of your mother's food, no?'

Umer nods.

'A taste you thought you'd never savour again?'

'Yes.'

'She must be worrying for you?'

'Yes.'

'You should go back.'

Umer looks at his companion, wondering, wondering who is this wizard who can read his mind?

'Uncle, how?'

So he tells him, about his own son who left home, in search of, 'who knows what?' We don't know anything about him. Except that he left home himself, he wasn't taken. Did we drive him out? Did we not do enough? Did we do too much? We don't know, but my wife took to her bed and won't leave it any more. And we have not found him. I only hope that someone found him. Someone good, who will look after him. And maybe, maybe he will return one day. My wife lives in hope, but I die a little every day that he is away.

'But, but ...' And Umer reveals his life to the old man who closes his eyes and listens, not passing judgement, only listening, carefully, weighing every word, seeming to caress every word, as though it were a precious stone. And when the story is done, he says nothing, nor opens his eyes. Till Umer thinks that he has fallen asleep. He is about to shake him, but Farooque gestures that he should be still.

'We are in need of a shikara boy, you know, one who is educated, can speak a little English. Would you like that?'

Now he peeps under his lashless eyelids and notes the wide toothy grin on the boy's face.

'We could also do with an extra good cook. Your mother makes good Kashmiri khana, does she?'

Another hopeful smile later and the old man talks about his own arthritic knees that prevent him from running to each of the four houseboats that are bursting at their seams with tourists right now. 'We need you,' he concludes.

'But, but, my mother will never allow me to ...'

'Come let's go now to her. I will talk to her. I may just be able to convince her, d'you think?'

Getting up with the old man's help, standing next to that agebent back, Umer now knows that he will convince his Ammi. That life may, just may become better after all.